Sawbones

By

Lawrence BoarerPitchford

ISBN: 0-9896629-2-6
ISBN-13: 978-0-9896629-2-5

DEDICATION

To the indomitable spirit of the United States, its citizens,
military, and civil servants. May that which makes our
country remarkable, carry us through hard times, so we
might be uplifted and enlightened. Be not so focused on
being unmovable, for it is the flexibility that makes us
strong, and our undying quest for compromise that builds
a nation.

CONTENTS

ACKNOWLEDGMENTS

NOTICE
Though some persons and places in this book are historical, the situations, and concepts are the sole invention of the author.

Credits:

Cover Artist ~ Lawrence BoarerPitchford

Senior Editor ~ Wendy Schirmer

Editor ~ Julie BoarerPitchford

CHAPTER 1

"This is the most damnable bad luck," Terence Miller mumbled under his breath as he made his way through the thick woods.

"Yanks shot my horse, I got this cut on my side, it's raining hard, and I got to be at Middleberg before ten this morn'en. Gumbo's going to kill me fer sure!"

The wind howled and the rain fell in a torrent, then stopped. Droplets plummeted from leaves and tree branches all around.

The sound masked his movements as he stepped around fallen trees and brambles. Pausing, he looked at a shadow in the darkness moving slowly through some bushes just ahead.

The outline betrayed it as a deer, and he knew that if circumstances were different he'd be having venison for breakfast come sunlight.

He watched the creature as it moved into a thicket and vanished from sight. For a moment he remained quiet, listening for movement. The soft crunching of hooves faded, and he again moved through the trees.

A stab of anger flared in his heart as he remembered his father and how they hunted coon and possum, fished in the muddy, and drank fresh shine. Anger filled him, for he'd never be able to do these things again with his pa.

The old man had gone off to fight the Yanks two years before. Terrence saw the tattered items that were brought back after the battle at Bull Run. The man that delivered his father's personal effects was also at the battle, and his words still lingered in Terrence's memory.

"Sorry' bout yer loss, Miss. You see, yer husband Filbert asked that if anything happen'd to him, that I'd bring his body back to ya fer burry'en here on yer land. But, that Yank cannon left not one hair off'n his head."

He looked down at his feet.

"I'waz next to em, and was laid out in like a sleep for some time. When I woke, it was like God had looked out fer me, but poor Filbert was gone. Only thing left were his boots, still standing side by side like he was still in em, and his satchel lying by them shoes."

"So I kept his things to bring back to ya. I'm awful sorry, but God is the one that decides these things not I."

The man looked up, tipped his hat to Terrence's mother, and walked back toward the white picket fence where he opened the gate. He climbed atop his horse and looked down at Terrence who was standing there, eyes wide with shock.

"You, boy... my advice to you is to get some revenge on them Yankees before this war is over and they've run off to Canada!"

The man again turned to the woman of the house.

"Miss," he said while tipping his hat.

He rode off down the dusty highway.

Terrence turned to his mother and shouted with rage.

"Them God damned Yanks will pay fer killing my pa!"

His mother walked over to him and pulled him to her.

"Yer only fifteen, and I won't see my son follow his father to the grave," she said with tears streaming down her cheeks.

She let him go and looked down. She was frail, with the consumption growing within her. The next year she died in her sleep after a bout of coughing.

Terrence was almost seventeen and now he was an orphan. His Uncle offered him a job in his store in town, and Terrence was about to oblige him when the Confederate army marched in.

He took up a place in line to join when fate intervened. A man who seemed on top of the world, with plenty of money in his pocket came around the corner.

The man looked at Terrence and remarked.

"Ya look like yer in need of honest work and a good meal. I need a man to help me track some escaped slaves. Are you that man?"

A whim took Terrence and he stepped out of line.

"What terms do you offer?" he asked.

Now Terrence laughed quietly to himself. "William Louise 'Gumbo' Whitman, not a dandy. Was near two years ago that you asked me to track them escaped slaves."

He stopped and thought.

Two years gone by now?

He removed his Penna Dutch hat and brushed his thick black hair back with his hand. After replacing his hat he pulled hard on his rubberize raincoat to shake the water off.

"Yup, two years. Seems like a hundred years," he whispered.

His rain slicker had kept his torso dry during the storm, but his trousers were soaked. His boots had clogged with mud several times as he moved across the farms and fields that dotted the landscape.

How'd those blue bellies move so fast along such terrain? No mind, I'll soon be done and be eating some bacon and biscuits, he thought while putting his hand on the leather satchel that hung down from his shoulder.

"They'll surely put up a statue of me," he said under his breath.

A pale glow began to illuminate the ground and the darkness abated slightly. Terrence could make out a large break in the forest ahead.

Stopping, he hunkered down and listened. All he heard were the falling droplets from the trees, and while that sound masked his movements, it could also be hiding the sounds of his enemies.

Pulling a Colt Dragoon pistol from its leather holster he cocked the hammer back. Working for Gumbo had trained him for this kind of business— to be overly cautious.

A few shots across the noses of those Unionist will keep their heads down and aims wild, so as to facilitate a hasty withdrawal, he thought to himself.

The smell of rotting leaves was ripe in the heavy

moist air and Terrence took two deep draws to see if any campfires were near. Only the rainy air and maybe a few fat old fungi were obvious… no smoke, no horses.

Listening again, he slowly turned his head from side to side. No sound, not even the wind.

Moving forward, he made it to the edge of the forest. It had taken him a good portion of the night to move from Calverton to Middleberg, but now he was nearing his goal. Another five miles, maybe less, and he'd be handing over the satchel and having a belly full of biscuits.

Stopping at the edge of the forest he could see a fog hanging heavy all about the cornfield. The corn was old, already picked and the stalks a dingy yellow.

Again he listened. In the distance there was a clanking sound, like a few tin cans clattering together. It was impossible to tell if it was a distant cowbell or soldiers on the march.

"Don't matter none," he said to himself, "too far off to see or hear the likes of me moving through this corn."

Crouching down, he moved across the open ground to the corn stalks. Slipping in to the field he took particular care to move down rows and only cross into other rows when necessary.

The mud was thick, and Terrence stopped to clean off his boot with a fallen cornstalk. The air was still.

White light was filling the sky, illuminating the fog and surrounding countryside in a dull milky color. The strong smell of earth and the hint of something strange in the air caused him to pause.

It was a familiar smell that he couldn't quite put his finger on it. Coffee, he thought as a bolt of terror shot up his spine. The sound of a man coughing echoed through the field. Then a shot rang out.

At first Terrence thought that he had slipped and fallen to the ground. But he quickly realized that he couldn't move his legs.

A burning feeling was inside him, but he couldn't stand or run. The Colt was lying in the mud just out of reach, and he heard the sound of shots being fired from all around.

The tromping of feet crunched through the corn stalks as he hid his face under his arms. Men in uniform were on both sides and all around. Then the volley of fire began.

The acrid smell of gunpowder filled the air, and debris rained down from every side. Cornstalks fell as if an invisible scythe were laying waste to the farmer's field.

The pain began to creep up his side. He didn't want to cry out, so he put his hand over his mouth. A man fell beside him… the side of his head was missing and the eye was hanging out of the socket.

Another body landed on top of him, convulsed, then rolled to the side. Cannon fire filled the air, and somewhere further away Terrence could hear the impacts throwing up dirt.

Men were crying and yelling all around. The ground was becoming sticky with blood.

"Lord God who art in heaven hallowed be thy name," Terrence said through clenched teeth, among the cacophony of prayers, pleading and wailing of the injured and dying.

"Please God make my legs work," he cried out.

CHAPTER 2

Carrigan LeRoy stepped outside the doorway of a dilapidated hay barn. Looking out into a gravel-covered roundabout he drew the damp air deeply into his lungs, and then exhaled heavily.

His six-foot frame cast no shadow in the cloudy morning light. Running his fingers through his thick black hair, he shut his eyes tightly. It seemed like a hundred years ago that he had left from Liverpool, and even longer since he'd become a doctor. Those were long days interning for Master Surgeon Sir John Hutchinson and Sir Benjamin Collins Brodie. The Royal College of Surgeons was the one of only a few places to get advanced training in surgical technique and applied medicine.

He had traveled home to speak with his father Lord Charles LeRoy. The man sat in his tweed house-coat in front of the fire.

"Carrigan my lad, you might take on a practice if you like or work for that fellow at the Kings College Hospital...what was his name?"

Carrigan sat for a moment admiring his father. The elder LeRoy was a full head shorter than Carrigan, but was stout and thickly muscled. He had a patch of graying hair along the sides of his head and a balding spot developing at the very top.

The senior LeRoy's dark blue eyes shone with thoughtful intelligence when charmed, and turned icy cold when provoked. Carrigan wanted to avoid provoking him.

"Reverend Lonsdale, Father," Carrigan said, the corners of his mouth turning up at his father's struggle to remember.

"Yes, yes! John Lonsdale the Reverend! He does seem a brooder if ever I've seen one." Charles chuckled softly. "A touch of spirits, my boy?"

"By your pleasure, Father," Carrigan said politely.

"Nonsense!" the elder clamored. "Such pomp betwixed father and son are absolved. As of today you are my equal."

He laughed, stood and fetched a decanter of brandy. Pouring two tumblers of scotch from the crystal container, he handed his son one of the glasses and knelt down by the fire.

For a moment he looked into the flames, then took the poker from its stand and prodded the burning logs.

"Most people prefer coal, but you can't get a better ambiance than a blazing fagot," he said.

"Now, regarding your future…" Charles continued, snapping Carrigan out of his thoughts. Replacing the poker, the senior LeRoy sat back into his chair.

"It is no small achievement to have followed the path of a surgeon. There a time when I was young that we called them barbers." He grinned.

"Barber-surgeons, Father," Carrigan corrected him.

"Yes, of course… barber-surgeons are what we used to call them."

"I plan on seeing the colonies. I'm going to the United States," Carrigan said as he raised the glass to his lips.

Nearly choking on his scotch, Lord LeRoy sat straight up on the edge of his seat.

"The colonies? For how long?"

"Not more than a year. I'll return after seeing the Island of Manhattan, the city of New York, and maybe even the town of Boston. I've developed quite an interest in those lands from reading Alexis DeToquville's Democracy in America. A fascinating read, and one I recommend." Carrigan sat back in his chair and put his boots near the fire to warm.

Laughing joyfully, Lord LeRoy took a long draft of scotch "You are quite a fellow for adventure my boy!" He shook his head. "I applaud your enthusiasm. You, as always, have my blessing."

"I suppose," Carrigan began, a mischievous grin on his lips, "that you should be glad that I didn't find Wuthering Heights as entertaining."

The senior LeRoy blustered. "A dreadful book – dreadful." Pausing for a moment to take another sip, he looked up at his son and laughed heartily again. "And written by a woman, no less!"

The two men discussed his coming trip late into the night. The talk lasted until the fire was only glowing red embers and the butler reminded Lord LeRoy that he should find some rest since he had a meeting with the Prime Minister later that morning.

Carrigan opened his eyes and surveyed the surrounding grasslands. The thoughts of his father pulled at his heart. He took out his pipe, stuffed it with tobacco, then struck a match on the rough wood of the barn. Taking several draws from the pipe, he let out a long stream of white smoke. In his mind's eye he saw the old study his father used - his father comfortably sitting near the fireplace turning pages of a book at a frightful pace. The man had an appetite for reading and consumed books on an hourly basis.

Carrigan remembered the first time he was asked to come into the den. His father was discussing business of the crown with Lord Bexely, when a messenger arrived.

Carrigan hid near the door behind a pillar of marble. He peeked out and watched his father break the seal on the letter and suddenly stagger to a chair.

Lord Bexely rushed to his side.

"What is it?" he asked, concerned.

"My wife, she's dead!"

His father's demeanor was shaken. The man's strength gone, his will broke like fragile glass.

Carrigan wanted to cry. True enough that his mother was now dead, but he knew that she had been ill for some time.

In his heart he was sure that she was in God's hands now. But to see his father, a man of unshakable resolve a tangled mess of bones and flesh, shook him to his core and he wept.

The elder's stature seemed diminished that day, and the man now appeared to Carrigan a frail little fellow in a chair.

"Be so kind as to find my son. Bring him to me so I might give this grievous news to him myself,"

Charles said.

"I'll find him," Bexely said as he turned to leave the den.

Lord Bexely slowly walked towards the doorway, then paused as he noticed Carrigan watching from his hiding place.

Seeing Bexely staring at him, Carrigan ducked behind the column. Bexely peered behind the support and looked down at Carrigan with a hint of anger and sadness.

"Spying on crown business is not becoming a Lord in training, young master," he said, his eyes narrowing. "Come with me, your father beckons you to him. But, I fear that you have cheated him of giving you this news himself."

His intense glare made Carrigan's feet move in the direction of the den. Once inside he dashed to his father, but stopped short remembering the LeRoy motto – to endure, to fight, to honor.

While standing there he became aware of the large room, and its two windows paned with leaded glass allowing in the fragile sunlight. Dust was suspended in the air, and his father's eyes were red from weeping.

"Still your heart, my boy," Lord LeRoy began as he looked at his son. "Your mother…" He choked up for a moment. "She is gone, she is gone…" His words fell into oblivion.

The rain stopped, and Carrigan looked down the dirt road leading to the barn. One of the litter bearers pushed past him.

"God damn, here comes another wagon," he said.

The sound of a wagon rolling up the road echoed

in the damp air. It approached quickly and pulled in front of the barn. The driver jumped down and rushed to the buckboard gate and untied it. Moans and sobbing came from the back.

"Another lot for ye, sir," the driver said, his husky voice shaken as he looked over at Carrigan.

"Was a skirmish not far from here... them renegade rebels trying to sneak across to Pennsylvania."

The sound of men in pain cut through the damp air as one of the unlucky called for his mother. The driver helped one man to his feet and down to the gray gravel road.

Congealed blood caked the end of the man's arm, severed at the elbow. His face betrayed his desperate attempt at controlling the savage pain as he held the stump aloft.

"Get to it, boys," Carrigan said to the litter bearers.

Both men dashed out and helped unload the wagon of its horrific contents. There was no end to pain here, and Carrigan said a silent prayer for the salvation of the poor men.

"This one didn't make it, Major," one of the litter bearers said as he looked in the wagon. "This one here can wait, and this one needs to be seen right away," the young man stated as if he were picking out a piece of meat from a butcher.

Carrigan wiped his hands on his blood-encrusted leather apron. His muscles ached, but he had to go on.

One more surgery, one more amputation, one more for the grave, he thought to himself. Then he muttered, "This is the end of days."

"What in God's name is going on here?" shouted

Major William Blake, as he stepped from the barn and next to Carrigan.

Standing six feet tall he was built like a blacksmith, and one of a dozen surgeons assigned to the field hospital. His black hair was parted at the side, and matted down with sweat.

He, too, wore a blood-covered leather apron. Turning to Carrigan, he almost smiled.

"Well, limy, we have work to do! Get back to your operating table. Litter bearers, get those wounded to the staging area." He did an about-face and re-entered the barn.

Carrigan followed Blake. The farm had become a field hospital and was covered with the wounded and dying.

The soldiers lay sprawled shoulder to shoulder on the dirt floor and propped up on any flat surface that could support a body. He stepped gingerly around the wounded, some with tears in their eyes, some with grimaces of pain that etched their faces with deep creases.

"Doc, the pain, the pain's unbearable," a shaky and shallow voice called.

Carrigan bent down, and in the low light could see a lieutenant whose leg had been removed just that morning. The man clutched the stump with both hands and looked beseechingly up at Carrigan.

Reaching into his leather pouch at his side Carrigan removed a small brown bottle marked 'Morphine'. Kneeling down, he pulled the tiny cork and held the bottle up to the Lieutenant's lips.

Close up, he could see the tears that lined the young man's face, and the tension etched in his jaw. But there was very little he could do now.

The man was either going to have a high fever and survive or die from the putrefaction.

"LeRoy! Get out here and lend a hand," the brash voice of Blake echoed from out back.

Putting the bottle away he stood and regarded the sprawled bodies laid in rows, then turned and headed out into the corral where the operating tables were.

The light was always better outside for performing surgery. Several large white awnings were erected to protect the patients from the rain, and Carrigan looked down the long line of wooden tables set up on raised platforms.

Blake was already at his table, a knife between his teeth and one in his right hand, a grim determined look on his face. He prepared to remove several finger on a mutilated hand.

The wounded were being brought through a gate at the side of the corral and laid out in the mud and dirt for triaging; done mostly by the deft eye of one of the surgeons who had an empty table.

Carrigan approached his operating table. Corporal Bizel stood there ready to assist him.

He knew this young man would closely watch his every move, for he was apprenticing to become a surgeon himself.

A soldier lay on top of the wooden planks that sufficed as a table. Holding aloft a soiled cloth in one hand and a tin bottle of chloroform in the other, Corporal Bizel appeared ready to administer the anesthetic.

Carrigan examined the wounded man noting that several mini-ball entrance wounds were present. He dreaded the exit wounds that were probably on the man's back.

Grabbing the soldier's shirt, Carrigan ripped it open and looked on the naked flesh. The wounds were grotesque purplish round holes with black centers.

"Apply the chloroform," Carrigan ordered.

Dabbing the chloroform onto the rag, the young soldier applied the dry side to the wounded man's face, allowing him to inhale the fumes. After a few moments the man's trembling body calmed, and Carrigan began the grisly work.

First he rolled the man onto his side. Examining the man's back he could see two exit wounds, large gaping craters oozing pink fluid.

"Three going in and three coming out," he stated. "Get me the sulfur powder."

Bizel quickly set down the chloroform and rag, and looked over the many bottles and tin containers sitting on a wooden plank atop two sawhorses. Finding a dented and rusty tin container, he unscrewed the top and handed it to Carrigan.

"Here ya go, Major," he said.

Taking the tin, Carrigan liberally shook out a fine mist of sulfur over the wounds both front and back. The smell of sulfur, blood, and torn meat was appalling.

Looking up, he saw Blake fast at work ramming a long metal probe into the wound of his patient.

Lost fragment perhaps, he thought as he turned his attention back to his own patient.

"More wagons," yelled a man near the barn.

"Bizel, set me up several suture needles and some catgut," he ordered.

Bizel quickly prepared the needles with fine silk thread.

"Here ya go, Major," he added as he held it aloft near the table.

"Now irrigate the wounds," Carrigan said.

Bizel took a bottle of water and poured it over the wounds. Carrigan quickly wiped it with a sponge and began sewing up one entry wound after another.

Moving quickly to the man's back he found some bone protruding.

"Forceps," he commanded.

Bizel quickly ran his hand over various instruments laid out on the plank and handed the tool to Carrigan.

"Here you go, sir," Bizel said as he moved back to the patient's head and retrieved his rag and chloroform.

The patient groaned loudly, and Bizel again applied the anesthetic to the man's face. Again, the patient fell silent and immobile.

Carrigan quickly removed the bone fragment and sewed up the seeping ligatures.

"Sponge," he said.

Bizel set down his bottle and rag and found the sponge sitting on the board. He wrung it out, poured water from the bottle on it, and wrung it out again.

"Use the water from my teapot," Carrigan commanded.

Bizel did as he was instructed and handed the sponge to the surgeon.

"No." Carrigan motioned with his head. "You wipe the wound; I need to finish sewing these holes shut."

For a moment Bizel looked excited, then his expression turned to anxiety, but he focused his attention on the patient and quickly cleaned the wound and stood back.

"Good fellow," Carrigan complemented. "Now, hand me the sulfur again."

Nimbly, he sewed up the last of the wounds and applied the yellow sulfur.

"I noticed, sir, that you applied the sulfur several times. What does it do?" Bizel asked.

"I read that when sulfur is applied, it retards the spread of infection. Why it does that, I'm not sure."

Bizel nodded and waited.

"This one is done!" Carrigan yelled to two privates standing by.

He looked over and saw more injured being placed in the corral.

"Bandage and put this man in the recovery tent," he said to Bizel.

"Yes, sir!"

Bizel quickly took some clean strips of old bed sheets and began wrapping them around the man's torso. When he was done, he motioned for the two privates to take the man to the white recovery tent at the far end of the barn.

Carrigan heard the sound of more wagons arriving, and he cursed under his breath.

"There's no end of them."

More soldiers on stretchers came from around the corner. He waited.

Looking up he saw that the morning was giving way to noon.

Just a moment to rest, that's all I ask.

Scanning the ground he saw the injured men laid out. They all needed a doctor, but not all needed a surgeon. Some could wait, and a few would wait too long; those would require the services of the mortician instead....

Resolutely, he motioned for a man dressed in civilian clothes to be brought up.

"Bring me that man and put him on the table," he said.

The litter bearers did as they were ordered, then quickly left to bring more broken men. Looking the man over, Carrigan saw the fellow was not much more than seventeen or eighteen. Clutched in his hands was a leather satchel.

"Damn," Blake angrily said. "Another for the grave!"

He wiped his brow with the back of his hand and then motioned for two soldiers to take the dead man away.

"Bring me another," he shouted.

Carrigan looked up and saw Blake standing there. Beyond the Major, the other surgeons worked furiously.

Blake looked to his left and then right. He spotted a man hunched over.

"You there, step up and let me have a look at your leg," he said.

"No!"

The young man clamored to his feet and made a limping run back towards the barn.

"You'll not have my leg," the soldier shouted back.

"Come here, you fool," Blake yelled.

Carrigan looked down at the boy with the bag, and took hold of the satchel. He pulled the bag away from the limp hands of the patient.

"No…" the young man mumbled. "Got to take it to gumbo…" his voice faded. "Middleburg… the Colonial Inn… they gonna put up a statue of me."

The boy took a short breath in, and then exhaled a

raspy sound; the death rattle of a fresh corpse. He was gone.

Bowing his head more from weariness than sadness, Carrigan closed his eyes for a moment. The sounds around him penetrated his mind and soul; the sound of insanity, cruelty, and helplessness.

Looking up, he called to the litter bearers again as they dropped off another man.

"Take this man to be embalmed."

More men tattered and savaged by battle were appearing now, streaming through and around the barn. Some staggered, and others were supported by fellow soldiers.

There seemed no end to them, as if some factory of horror had been created to produce with great efficiency sick and shattered men.

"Give me that man there," he pointed to an unconscious man who was bleeding from his head and chest.

CHAPTER 3

Billy Louise "Gumbo" Whitman had just put his cards on the table when he ran his stubby fingers through his sweaty blond hair. He smiled across the table at his opponents.

"Ace high, fellas."

He pulled a thin cigar from his pocket, removed a match from a box sitting on the table next to his pistol, and chuckled like a man who knew something funny.

He struck the match and watched the flame burn brightly. He took two long draws from the cigar and exhaled the purple acrid smoke into the air.

"Well I'll be damned to hell!" Walter Pitman said as he took off his derby and wiped his brow with his handkerchief.

Walter was a short stocky man with a wreath of black hair about his otherwise balding head. His face was dirty, and his hands too, and he had wrestled with the idea of calling Gumbo a cheat, but common sense dictated otherwise. So he pushed away from the table and stood up.

"You're a hell of a card player, Gumbo," Walter said while shaking his head.

Putting his hat back on, he turned towards the bar.

"I need a beer after that mess!" He laughed.

Tossing a half-dollar on the table Gumbo grinned up at Pitman.

"Fetch us both a beer," he said, more like an order rather than a request.

Walter looked down at the money. His blood boiled when Gumbo would behave like this. But, true to form he just picked up the half-dollar.

"Sure, Gumbo… you're the muleskinner here."

Gumbo savored his cigar as he looked around the table at the remaining players.

The man to his right, Billy Preston, had been riding with Gumbo since he was twelve. Billy, now sixteen, looked sickly.

His eyes looked out from deep black sockets with no emotion. Even the boy's hair appeared sickly as it hung down to his shoulders, greasy and black as coal. But the boy was quick with a gun, and not with his wits, and that made him valuable to Gumbo.

The next man was Jack Gable. A brute of a man, muscled like a bear, he was not easy to control and pretty much did as he pleased.

His hair was cropped short and he had a full brown mustache that hung down below his chin on either side. Jack was the complete opposite of Preston; a fanatic about keeping clean and tidy. He was rumored to have shot a barber for not cleaning the razor before commencing with a shave.

Sitting to Gumbo's left was a man that scared him. Peter "Coffee Cup" French had gotten his nickname after drowning a Chinaman in a large caldron of coffee. When asked why, Coffee Cup just said, "The man failed to ask me if I wanted cream with my coffee."

Though Coffee Cup was arrested, he escaped and found his way to Louisiana where he made his living as a bare-knuckles boxer for a while until he met up with Gumbo and his bounty hunters.

Coffee Cup looked over at Gumbo with his dark blue eyes that bore deep into a man's soul. Narrowing his eyes, Coffee Cup reached over and took the second cigar from Gumbo's pocket.

Putting the smoke into his mouth, he sneered.

"Now Gumbo, what is it that you got planned for us now? We been sitting in this here hotel for neigh on one week with no work. We'll surely be out of money soon with nothing but the smell of whores and rotten rye to show for it."

"I told you all that Terrence is bringin' the work. He'll be here when he's here. You fellas been eating like dandies, drinking like cowboys, and whoring like senators. I fail to see why you're bellyaching," chided Gumbo.

"Terrence? That boy's as good for nothing as I've seen. He's probably leapt off to California by now," Coffee Cup said while getting up from the table. "If he don't show up by tomorrow, I'll have to reevaluate our partnership."

Coffee Cup turned and walked past Pitman, who was returning. Coffee bellied up to the bar.

"Whisky," he said.

"What's digging in his craw?" Walter asked while setting down Gumbo's beer next to him.

"Nothing. He's tired of sitting here waiting, and

losing his money to me," Gumbo said.

"When we gonna get us another run away nigra?" Billy asked. "Them jobs paid us well in the past."

"We have bigger fish in the pan, boy," Gumbo angrily stated. Lowering his voice, he said, "Them gray coats dun give us some money to wait here, and them fellas aint the forgetting type. When he gets here and gives us the message, and we do the job proper, we'll get a lot more money than we've been getting."

"We can take another job after that. Hell, them runaways are always needing to be brought back."

Billy shrugged his shoulders and looked down at the table.

"Was just wondering," he added.

"Stop yer worrying. This job's gona be the best, and all of you," he pointed around the table, "will make a hundred dollar-apiece when it's done."

Walter drank down his beer.

"I'm gonna go over to Madam Pinwheel's house. Them sporting gals sure smell nice," he said as he put down his glass and made for the door.

Gumbo turned to see Coffee Cup make for the door also.

"Well, get to yer business, the rest of you," he said to the remaining group.

Jack and Billy stood up and headed for the door. For a moment Billy seemed hesitant to leave, but fostering a backward glance at Gumbo, he stepped outside into the bright light of the street.

Gumbo looked around the saloon. Mostly locals, and displaced country folk were drinking or playing cards.

He was getting tired of waiting. Terrence was four days late already, and Gumbo was beginning to worry that the Confederates would return and demand their advance back. Then there would be a bit of nastiness, since they'd spent most of it already.

They'll just have to understand that it was for expenses, he thought.

He tipped his beer mug up to his lips and drank. Then he stood up and put his pistol into its holster, and picked up his hat from the table. "Madam Pinwheel is a peach of a lady," he said, as he opened the saloon door and stepped out into the light..

CHAPTER 4

Finally the last of the injured had arrived. The daylight had faded, and the onset of darkness was threatening to stop all surgery.

Carrigan finished swabbing the bloody edges of a bayonet wound. His table was soaked through with blood, and his boots were covered.

Quickly sewing up the inner tissue, he then sutured the outer wound. Doing this for both the entry and exit, he set down his needle and rested heavily against the wooden table that held his surgical tools, drugs, and bandages.

"That's all, Major," Bizel said, as he helped the stretcher bearers put the soldier on the litter.

Picking up a bucket of murky looking water, Bizel began scrubbing down the wooden planks, dislodging the clotted blood and bits of matter. He cleaned every inch.

Finally, he doused the table with the bucket, letting the bloody water fall between the gaps and onto the soil below.

"You're sure there's no more?" Carrigan asked.

Bizel smiled. "That's it, Major," he said wearily.

Turning, Carrigan looked at the pile of body parts lying in a heap between the operating platforms.

Blake was standing at his station, that same grim look on his face. Lifting a pipe to his lips he inhaled, making the tobacco glow in the dimming light.

"Well, LeRoy, old chap," he began, "what say you and I have a sip of whisky before we call the day done?"

"Sounds like a very good idea," Carrigan said as he turned to leave.

Stopping, he noticed the leather satchel from the morning. "Blimey, I forgot to give this to the lads when they took that civilian this morning."

"Not to worry your limy head," Blake said, as he walked over to him.

"We'll just drop it off tomorrow. Perhaps they'll not have buried him yet, or better yet, the family will provide a reward for the return of the body and satchel?"

Blake nearly licked his lips with the thought of extra money.

"All, I want to think about right now is a stiff drink and a soft cot." Carrigan sighed.

Picking up the satchel, he tucked it under his arm and stepped into the bloody grass. As he walked towards the barn, he noted the soft glow of a lantern that had been lit to ward off the darkness.

It was a universal truth, that dying men feared the dark, and it was a saintly kindness to abate that fear. Carrigan knew many of those men he had worked on today would be dead by the light of morning.

He and Blake made the walk to the officers' tents in silence. The path led them past the enlisted men's tents, and Carrigan heard the sounds of mouth harps and jugs being played.

The words to the song were not clear, but he saw men dancing about - celebrating their victory over death.

"Sorry I don't have any rum to offer you, Englishman," Blake said. "But some fine American bourbon will warm your heart and stiffen your spirit." He puffed his pipe as he spoke.

Ahead, Carrigan saw several men gathered at the officer's tents. They had already set up a table and were sitting in chairs playing cards. On the table were several jugs and bottles, some of which were actually labeled.

Opening the flap to his tent, Carrigan went in. The small white cabin tent was modest in size, measuring only twenty feet by twenty feet.

A center pole propped up the ceiling, and the floor was a set of wooden planks. Along one wall sat a cot covered with a blue woolen army blanket.

A small desk with chair was sitting against the other wall. From the center pole hung down an oil lantern.

Going to the desk, he removed a box of matches, struck one, and ignited the wick of the lantern. The inside of the tent was bathed in an orange hue.

Adjusting the wick, the small yellow flame bobbed up and down causing the shadows to twist and contort.

"Come on, limy!" Blake called from outside. "There's money to be made out here from these map drawing bastards!"

"Better to have a pen in my hand than a knife – sawbones," one of the men shouted from the card table.

Laughter erupted, and Carrigan heard Blake harrumph.

"I'll be out in a moment," he called back, as he tossed the leather satchel onto his cot and changed his clothes.

Stopping just at the tent door, he looked at the leather pouch, then shrugged his shoulders and stepped outside.

The night was not cold, but cool. In the sky were clouds, occasionally obscuring the sliver of a moon that had begun its climb in the sky.

The caw from the ravens echoed loudly in the darkness, and Carrigan cringed at the thought of what they were feasting on.

"Here ya go, John Bull. Have a swig of this tar juice to warm those tired bones!"

Blake handed Carrigan a tin cup filled with bourbon.

Taking a drink, Carrigan felt the burning liquid running down his throat and into his empty belly. A stabbing pain struck him, and he felt as though he would collapse.

"Seems that our map making friends here have a whole plate of Johnny Cakes," Blake pointed out. "Be top rail fellows and let us have a few."

Turning slightly, Captain Baum removed his pipe from his mouth and laughed heartily.

"You parlor soldiers want some corn dodgers? It aint steak and kidney pie."

He nodded his head like a man who understood the feeling after hard work.

"You two look played out if ever I've seen anyone down-in-the-mouth." Picking up the plate, he handed it to Blake.

"Don't choke on it. I'd hate to see you dead when I've heard that the war is nearly over."

"You say that every time I see you," Blake said, as he stuffed two corn biscuits into his mouth. Handing the plate to Carrigan, he washed down his meal with the cup of bourbon.

"Not just gossip," Baum said as he shuffled a deck of cards. "Seems that there are talks going on right now about surrender."

"Baum, you keep talking like that and I might just kiss you." Blake laughed, as did the rest of the men at the table.

Carrigan took a corn dodger and put it into his mouth. Chewing slowly he could feel his fatigue catching up.

"Mind if we sit?" Carrigan politely asked.

"Get him," laughed Baum pointing his thumb up at Carrigan. "Sit, Englishman, if you're not afraid that your card playing will end up like the battle at Chippawa…"

Pulling up a chair Carrigan sat down, put some coins on the table, and waited for the cards to be dealt. He watched the deft hands of Baum tossing the cards around to each man… Captain Harris, Major McHilt, Lieutenant Fitzwater, Captain Reed, Major Blake, Carrigan, and lastly Baum. It took only a minute to deal out the five cards to each player and when he was finished, Baum took a long drag from his pipe and blew a smoke ring across the table.

"Let's draw upon good faith, friends, and their loose pocketbooks," Baum said with a wicked grin.

An old hoot owl called from somewhere in the

night. Carrigan removed his silver pocket watch from his shirt pocket, pressed the latch, opened the timepiece, and held it close to the lantern; it was ten to midnight. Closing the lid, he replaced it in his shirt pocket.

"I've had it," he said somberly. "It's late and I bid you gentlemen a good night."

Blake looked up at Carrigan.

"You sure are a sore winner." He laughed. "Oh well, seems we'll not win back any of that silver the limey's leaving with. So let's just finish this bourbon and bay at the moon, boys!"

Standing, Baum eyed Carrigan for a moment. Boasting a chuckle he slapped Carrigan on the back.

"I guess I underestimated you Englishman. You're quite a downy card player."

Sitting back down, he struck a match and put the fire to the tobacco in his pipe. Puffing softly, he regarded the men sitting at the table.

"Suppose we should all hit the cots. Tomorrow will be another long day."

Carrigan turned and headed to his tent. There he pulled back the flap and entered. Sitting down on his cot he realized that there was something uncomfortable under his bum.

Leaning to one side, he removed the leather satchel from under him and stared at it in the low lamplight. Slowly he undid the buckle.

Opening it, he dumped the contents out onto the cot. To his surprise there was quite a lot. Brass percussion caps glinted in the weak light. A powder flask filled with powder and detailed in silver scrolling lay on its side. Loose balls of lead were strewn about across his dark blue blanket.

Carrigan poked his finger around the various papers until he noticed a wax-sealed document. Taking it, he examined it close to the lantern.

The seal was done in green, and the stamp appeared smooth with no markings. Putting it on his desk, he sat down on the cot again. Opening one of the papers, he looked it over carefully.

The letter had been written in a steady hand and consistently flourished on each cursive loop. Noting the contents to be a love letter, he sighed heavily knowing that the intended girl would be devastated when she heard the news of the boy's death.

Picking up a piece of rolled paper, Carrigan unrolled it and noted it's writing to be much different. This document explained that Gumbo would be waiting for the courier at a place called the Western Colonial Inn in the town of Middleburg. It explained that the wax document should be delivered to him.

Holding up the sealed document one more time, Carrigan viewed it from all angles, slowly turning it in his hand.

"Probably another letter concerning a tryst or such," he reasoned.

Putting it and the other contents back into the satchel, Carrigan set the pouch on his desk and disrobed. He dressed in his nightshirt, pulled back the blanket, blew the lantern out, and crawled into bed.

Outside he heard the revelry of the enlisted men as he faded into sleep.

CHAPTER 5

"Them rebs is on the run," shouted someone from afar.

Sitting up on his cot, Carrigan slowly got to his feet, then stopped. Smiling, he realized that it must've been only a dream.

"Two corps have driven them Johnny's into the river at Appomattox; get up, ya sorry excuses for solders," came the voice again.

Carrigan quickly stripped off his nightshirt and pulled on his dress shirt, blue trousers, socks and boots. He stumbled outside his tent.

The sky was gray, and there was the scent of rain in the air. In the distance he saw the smoke from the cook stoves rising into the air, and all around him, other soldiers were emerging from their tents looking just as confused as he was.

Galloping through the camp was a messenger on the back of a dark black horse. The fellow looked bedraggled, as if he had little sleep or food recently. Rounding one of the roads, he came towards Carrigan at a trot.

Blake dashed from his tent and scooped up the cavalryman's reins and held his horse fast. The poor lad nearly flew from the saddle as Blake shouted up at him.

"If this is a prank, and at this hour of the morn, you'll be tarred and feathered for this!"

Regaining his composure, the young man in the saddle jerked the reins from Blake and scowled down at him.

"No prank, sir! Telegraph report came in this morn. Them rebs have up and left Petersburg and are moving out past Appomattox river," he said excitedly. "The damndest thing to be seen!"

"What the devil? Any casualties?" Blake demanded.

"No, sir! Lee just up and left. Lee's been bested by Grant and he knows it. I'm on my way to deliver this message to all the units from here to Washington. Now, outta my way," the young man said as he spurred his horse and raced out along the eastern road.

Blake raised his eyebrows, then put his pipe into his mouth. Lighting a match he puffed on the pipe until the tobacco glowed red.

Looking over at Carrigan, he shrugged his shoulders.

"Seems Baum might have been right. And it galls me."

"Right about what?" Baum asked while walking up and pulling on his blue jacket.

"Seems we're on the verge of winning this war," Blake added.

Baum looked at him for a moment with a blank

expression.

Carrigan felt his heart leap to his throat. To win the war would mean he could finally go home and try to put all this horror behind him.

Finally he'd get a rest that would not consist of three parts liquor and one part fatigue. A good night's sleep in the English country, in an English bed – and he would sleep for a week.

"You're shitting me!" Baum laughed. "That's the best news I've heard all morning!"

"LeRoy," called Blake. "Get properly dressed and we'll go into Middleburg and get us a good hot meal for breakfast. If there ain't no casualties, we deserve a righteous meal! What is that little inn called there?"

Baum laughed.

"You surely don't have a head for names Blake; that inn is called the Colonial Inn – and they don't take too kindly to rabble like you dining in their establishment."

Baum pulled down on the corners of his jacket to straighten it.

"But with me along, they'll clearly see that my sophistication will eclipse your ignorance, and they will not take us for a couple of Bummers."

Rolling his eyes, Blake looked over at Carrigan.

"What do you think, limey? Shall we keep company with this line-drawer?"

Carrigan smiled. "Sure – he's nearly as upstanding a fellow as the two of us."

"Yer lucky Baum that Carrigan thinks so highly of you. Come along as you will, and try not to slow us down."

"I'll inform the orderlies that we'll be out for the day. I'm sure that Doc Eckart and Doc Billings will be willing to keep an eye on things here until our return," Carrigan said.

"We've done the same for them on plenty of occasions."

"Well, fine and good," Baum said. "Let's waste no more time. Each to his own tasks and we'll meet back here… saddle up and be off."

Flipping open his pocket watch, Carrigan noted that it was seven in the morning. To find and ask Doctor Eckart and Billings took only ten minutes, and to get dressed took only another ten.

Carrigan doused the palm of his hand with some cologne, then rubbed his hands together and applied the liquid to his face and neck.

Retrieving his hat from the back of his desk chair he noticed the brown leather satchel sitting on his desk.

"Middleburg," he said out loud. "Colonial Inn."

He grabbed the satchel and slipped the strap over his head and shoulder; letting the satchel hang down at his right side, just above his holster. He adjusted it for comfort.

Making sure that his cravat, shirt, jacket, pants, and hat all made him look well groomed, he took up his billfold and left the tent.

"Grace of God!" said Baum from high in the saddle. "You're a fancy English dandy if ever I've seen one!"

Carrigan took up the reins of his horse, stepped into the stirrups, and climbed into the saddle. After making sure his jacket was straight, he looked back at Blake and Baum and motioned forward.

At a walk, they moved down the eastern road towards Middleburg. The surrounding countryside bustled with wagons and men.

Soldiers were in every direction as they left camp. Following the road as it turned slightly south, Carrigan noticed the farmlands on either side. Small plots of corn, or wheat, or rye were waving in the subtle breeze, and in the gray sky he could see several black ravens riding the currents of air.

He focused back on the road and maneuvered around a convoy of cannons being towed towards Petersburg.

"Them rebs will be begging Grant to surrender soon I think," Baum said loudly over the noise of the wagons and marching soldiers.

"Not soon enough if you ask me," Carrigan said. "Not nearly soon enough."

CHAPTER 6

The town of Middleberg was not more than ten miles from the farm-turned-field hospital. Carrigan, Blake, and Baum casually made their way north up the Richmond and Petersburg road.

Carrigan took a moment to view the controlled chaos. Many soldiers moved up and down the road, and mule trains towed wagons filled to the gunnels with larder supplies and ammunition.

Fit men marched south, while the walking wounded staggered north. The road was littered with animal dung, discarded empty tin cans, and in some places, bloody rags and bandages. Every now and then a guard post was set up, staffed with old and young men alike, halting traffic and inquiring as to the purpose of the traveler's passage.

Seeing several young men with Spencer rifles at a guard post, Carrigan commented to Blake.

"He's carrying one of those new rifles that can repeat," he pointed.

"No doubt it will make our labors more the

furious," Blake said solemnly.

"Halt," called the young private as he held up his hand and stood in the way of their horses.

"What outfit are you from and where are you going?"

I'm Major LeRoy, and these two men are Major Blake and Captain Baum. We're from the Lucas Farm, Union field hospital. We're heading to Middleberg to exercise one or two bottles of whisky."

"Yer a funny talker, mister," the private said while looking at his two companions.

"Be on yar guard. There's been Confederate cavalry raiders about making mischief. We've got orders to shoot on sight anyone trying to bypass the road or enter without cause."

The young private eyed the three mounted men, then stepped aside and motioned them forward.

"Get along, sirs," he said as they passed.

"Seems we're taking on anyone who's just come into puberty," Blake said with a shake of his head.

Gray mud churned underfoot as the horses tromped along toward Middleberg. A light dew covered their woolen uniforms, saddles, and horses.

On the road, mixed with the steady stream of supply wagons headed south, civilians intertwined. Every so often, Carrigan would see a farmer, tradesman, or couple in a buggy, coming and going from Middleberg. No doubt, Carrigan thought, coming from, or going to some farm nearby.

Up ahead he could see the outskirts of the town filled by the large number of soldiers who had swelled the Union ranks in the past two years.

Entering, they moved along the main street. Carrigan noticed the cramped buildings on either side.

Stores were prominent with their richly painted signs, shingles and trim.

Homes appeared, placed down side streets, or between businesses. Ahead he could see a three-story building with a sign across the top of the second floor— the words 'Western Colonial Inn' painted in black against a white-washed background.

"Ah, here we are…" Baum said, steering his horse to a hitching post.

"A fine establishment with fine whisky to wash this road dust from my throat!"

"Yes, yes the road dust indeed," Blake added. "What about you, LeRoy? Ready for a drink of Middleberg's finest spirits?" He laughed loudly.

"Middleberg's finest whisky couldn't be worse than that whisky from that distillery near Harmony Grove last year," Carrigan said. "But whisky with breakfast?"

"Whisky is good anytime." Baum looked indignant.

"Then, whisky, beer, eggs, bacon, and biscuits it is," Blake declared. "I could eat a mule."

"You just might," Baum said with a wink of his eye. He looked around at the many people in the streets.

"Where's the livery in this blasted town?"

"You're right, not wise to leave our horses on the street. Perhaps we should ask," Blake said.

"You!" Baum called to a young boy dressed in brown knee pants and a white shirt striped in black. "Where's the Livery here?"

The boy stopped and for a moment and looked as if he was not sure what a livery was. Carrigan saw his little eyes sparkle with a thought as he spoke.

"Back the way you come, sir, and make a right. You can't miss it – it's the new building that's not quite finished. The big sign says Beam and Guthrie livery, wheel right, and blacksmith."

The boy began fidgeting with his shirt as if he was brushing off some dirt.

"It burned down two years ago. They just rebuilt it."

"Thank you, boy," Baum said. "Come here and I'll give you an Indian Head penny."

Nearly jumping out of his skin, the boy rushed to get to Baum. His feet stumbled and he fell with a thud into the dirt.

Sheepishly standing, he dusted off his breeches and made an embarrassed smile. Holding up his hand he waited for Baum to fish out a penny from his leather coin purse and hand it to him.

Carrigan chuckled as the boy took the coin, his eyes wide with gratitude and greed.

"Thank you, sir," the boy said as he put the coin into his pocket. "I'm going to buy a peppermint stick!"

He ran off towards the general store.

Baum chuckled at the boy's youthful excitement, then turned his horse and began to ride back down the street. Blake and Carrigan also laughed and followed Baum towards the stables.

"Now, LeRoy old fellow, what is that satchel at your side? I've not seen it on you before and it doesn't look like the Army's given it to you."

"One of my patients who died yesterday," Carrigan began. "He seemed to be a local who stumbled into one of those pitched battles. Killed by two mini-balls. But he said something about his next of kin being here in Middleburg and getting this satchel to him."

"Next of kin?" Blake said as they approached the livery. "Now Mr. LeRoy, you are a naive fellow. Have you even looked inside that satchel to see if you're not aiding the enemy?"

"Enemy?" The thought never entered his mind.

"Yes – enemy," Blake stated again. "The man could have been a courier for them gray britches."

"In fact, I did look through the belongings and nothing seemed out of the ordinary. But my intent was to discover the identity of a next-of-kin, that's all."

Carrigan dismounted and took up his horse's reins.

"When we get to the inn, you'd better let me have a look at that bag. We'd not want to deliver a message to Johnny Reb, if we can avoid it," Blake said.

Carrigan turned his horse over to the livery hand, paid the fee, got his receipt, and began walking back to the hotel with his friends.

They turned onto Main Street and navigated the ruts and mud holes that made up the road. After a short walk, they arrived at the Western Colonial Inn.

At the door, Carrigan stomped soundly on the porch decking, knocking off the mud from his boots. Then he lifted the latch and entered the establishment.

CHAPTER 7

Immediately to his left was a set of stairs. Carrigan saw on either side of the entry were rooms. On the left was a dining room, and on the right was a parlor and bar. He looked inside the parlor and noted a few people standing at the bar.

The tavern keeper looked over at them with a curious eye. Carrigan saw the man was not small, for his muscles bulged under his collared shirt. He wore an apron, and at his elbows were garters just below his large biceps.

The man reached up and twisted the ends of his black mustache.

"You here for the bar or breakfast?" he asked.

"Breakfast," Baum said. "And we'd like to get drinks in the dining room."

"Of course," the burly man replied. "You can sit anywhere you want. I'll have the cook start making your food."

Carrigan noted the man walked with a limp. Clearly he wore but one boot, and the clacking sound against the wood floor indicated the man sported a wooden peg-leg.

He limped with ease as he moved from the bar to the hallway, to the dining room, and finally the kitchen. The three men found a table near the middle of the room and sat down.

Carrigan put his napkin on his lap, adjusted his silverware, and sat back. All waited for their drinks.

Soon the barkeep came from the kitchen.

"Biscuits are about ready, and the cook is fixing eggs, pork chops, bacon, and steak, with fried potatoes. Now what can I get you three gentleman from the bar?"

"Bring us a bottle of Monongahela and three glasses, and a pail of beer," Carrigan said as he looked about the room.

The wallpaper was red with gold filigree, and showed fruits and berries all swirled together in a repeated pattern. Oil lanterns sat on shelves mounted to the walls, and candles were present on every table.

Hanging from the ceiling, spaced evenly along the length of the room, he saw two large chandeliers with many lamps cradled in wrought iron rings. The other tables were covered in white cloth with dining implements set out.

There were a set of windows on one side that faced an ally, and across was the remains of what looked to be a burned down house.

"Here you go, gentlemen," the bartender said, as he hobbled back into the room.

In his arms he carried three short beer glasses, a pail of beer, an emerald green glass bottle fitted with a porcelain stopper, and three tumbler glasses.

Setting down the empty glasses first, he then bent

down and put the whisky bottle on the table, and then placed the beers in front of each man.

He brushed off his apron, took a rag from his pocket, and swabbed out the whisky glasses.

"I think you'll enjoy this whisky. It's a fine brand," he said, as he opened the bottle and poured some of the contents into each glass.

Holding it up, Carrigan swirled the amber liquid around once and admired the color. Sniffing it, he could tell it was a good vintage: ten years old, maybe fifteen.

He took a sip. "Very smooth to the palate," he declared, as he set down his glass and took a long draft from his beer.

"It should only be a few more minutes before you're served," the barkeep said. "Anything else I can get for you?"

"No," Baum stated. "But check back in a half hour to see if we need another bottle of Monongahela."

"When we need another bottle, you mean," Blake corrected as he drank down his whisky and refilled his glass.

Watching the bartender leave, Carrigan sat admiring the room.

"That satchel if you please," Blake said holding out his hand.

As he held them out, Carrigan scoffed at the thought of the documents in the bag being treasonous. "Don't lose any of the items in there. They're somebody's property and not ours."

"Property?" Baum finished his beer and set the glass on the table.

"That satchel is the property, and responsibility, of the Union Army… and these United States."

Several boys and a woman arrived carrying plates of food. The woman was not attractive.

Her plain face was long and her nose wide. Her black hair was mussed and tied behind her head in a bun of dark curls.

Her clothes, a voluminous skirt of light yellow flowers and light blue cotton, was covered in front by an apron. The dress flowed about as she walked, colliding with empty chairs and ballooning out at times.

She rushed over to the table and set down a disc of stone, and atop that a large black skillet of biscuits. The boys brought plates filled with eggs bacon, and pork chops.

Stopping one of the boys from leaving, Blake asked him to fetch another pail of beer for the table.

Carrigan watched Blake and Baum tuck their linen napkins into their shirt collar; a lowbrow trait he'd not gotten used too. He picked up his fork and knife.

Near the biscuits were several jars of honey, a small plate with a scoop of butter, and two jars of jam. In the middle of the table he saw salt and pepper shakers made of glass and topped with tin lids.

He removed two thick biscuits and set them on his plate, then scooped out two fried eggs.

The biscuits erupted with steam as he cut off the crusty brown tops, and liberally applied some churned white butter and a blob of honey.

The boy returned with the pail filled with sudsy beer. Without a word, he retreated back to the kitchen.

Blake took the pail and poured a liberal amount into his own glass. Lifting his fork and knife, he began his assault on his breakfast.

"So?" Blake asked as he shoveled a large fork of eggs into his mouth.

"What possessed you to butt into this fellow's business and personally return his property to his relatives?"

Baum laughed. "You should have left it to the embalmer. That fellow rifles pockets for a living."

Carrigan lifted a fork full of potatoes to his mouth and chewed, swallowed, and drank a small amount of beer.

"Seemed reasonable. We were, after all, coming to the very town in which the man was going."

"You are a strange breed, Englishman," Baum declared as he carried a chunk of biscuit to his mouth.

"Not strange, Mr. Baum, but considerate," Carrigan corrected.

"What will you do if the dead fellow has no kin here in Middleburg?" Blake casually asked.

"That obstacle I shall overcome when it is presented." Carrigan smiled as he reached for his beer and drank another small amount. "Besides, I shan't let such ranker ruin my first civilized breakfast in a month."

"Quite right of you to say that," Blake responded, as the table fell silent and the three men ate.

Soon the plates were empty and each man in turn pushed away from the table. Baum struck a match and ignited his pipe. Taking a long drag, he puffed smoke rings into the air.

Blake removed two cigars, offered one to Carrigan, and struck a match. All three men sat quietly as they enjoyed the rich tobacco from their respective sources.

"Hand me that sack," Blake requested, and

Carrigan did. "Interesting," Blake murmured as he stuck in his meaty hand and rifled through the contents. "Seems that this fellow was remarkably common."

Setting the satchel on the table, Blake dumped out the contents.

"A watch, some letters, caps, powder flask, ball shot, a receipt for gumbo, and a sealed note," he observed. "Look here, the boy must have been sent to acquire some gumbo from a local eatery; most likely for his family."

He picked up the sealed note. "It's not addressed to anyone. It could have come to me, and I opened it by mistake."

"True enough," Carrigan confirmed as he exhaled some dark purple smoke into the air.

"But, I must add that the dying man something about taking it to gumbo."

Blake smiled. "You would be daft to take it to gumbo, which I know to be a soup made in Louisiana. I have to say that the man was just mumbling nonsense to you, Carrigan old chap!"

"That may be so," Carrigan agreed. "Very common for a dying man to see and say many things that may not be logical."

"Therefore," Blake said as he raised his butter knife, "Baum, be a good fellow and remove the chimney of that lamp."

Baum took his napkin and with it grabbed the chimney of the lamp and held it to the side. Blake swiftly put the blade of his butter knife into the flame and heated it.

Setting the letter down flat on the table, he slipped the hot knife through the wax seal separating it from the bottom half of the letter.

"It appears that you have done this sort of 'dagger heating' before?" Baum cocked his head. "It is most ungentlemanly to read another's mail," Blake said while unfolding the letter. "But, when in rouge's company…"

He looked over the letter.

"Well?" Carrigan said, taking a sip of his whisky.

"Most curious indeed," Blake commented.

"Don't be a raving jackass," Baum said. "Read it out loud or hand it around!"

"Very well," Blake said.

He held the letter at arm's length and narrowed his eyes.

"Dear Charles," he began. "Robert over by Elderbrook ran to Tim Orderly Dupree down toward Orebow. Let every available vice end. Cheat if the yearning panders on in no time waiting in the hearth for a tall, healthy, eager rascal." He looked about the table before continuing.

"Susan pretends everything needs darning in night gayety. Therefore, we ordered David a yard stick and to calculate a pitiful instance that aroused Lana. Take routs available veering elegantly, lingering in no gaps."

"Bring yearning to Randy's account in Nassau. Tip often, getting all instances naturally settled. Ask pork riding ills lasting, to hide in rear dike. In no time everything resembled Calvin's exceptional pittance typifying all nonsense, drafted, down every little initial variable entered routinely."

Blake took a drink from his whisky glass. He cleared his throat and finished the letter.

"To our great opus, on Susan's elegance, Calvin requested every exceptional kindness bringing righteous indignation, devoid gathering empathy. Mostly I digress, not interested goading hot tempered angels. Please return ill labored, 5."

"Looks as though Charles has a mad mother or sister." Baum chuckled.

"Perhaps," Blake said as he continued examining the letter.

"It is written well, with a steady hand, but the sentences are odd and confused in their grammar. The words make little sense as if written by a child."

"Maybe it's his young sister or daughter," Carrigan suggested.

"The writing is too neat," Blake said.

"Then a code of some sort?" Carrigan offered up.

"Yes," Baum stated as he poured more beer into his glass. "Hand that to me."

Blake passed the letter to Baum who examined it for a long while.

"It's clearly a coded letter. No one in their right mind would write like this."

"So what is the cipher?" Carrigan asked.

"Let me see…"

Baum took the stem of his pipe and touched the end of his chin.

"It's set up to read like a simple cryptograph." He paused. "And not very well done one, I might add. It seems that the first letter of each of the words when put together makes a word."

"Well, what does it say?" Blake huffed.

"Let me see… Robert Todd to leave City Point with Father. Spending two days at Capital. Traveling by train to Gaines April third. Intercept and deliver to Goose Creek Bridge midnight April fifth."

He sat back puffing on his pipe looking pleased

with his recitation. Suddenly, he looked at Carrigan and Blake.

"Good God, they mean to abduct the president's son, Captain Robert Lincoln!"

CHAPTER 8

Gumbo sat atop his mount and waited in the brush just off the road. No doubt some witless locals would be along any time.

Coffee Cup, Jack, and Billy were across the road waiting for his signal. Walter was just behind him, and hidden behind a tangle of briers.

Little traffic passed along the road that day and Gumbo was beginning to think that they should just pack it in and head back to the town, when he heard the clopping of hooves approaching.

They had spent through their advance already and were in need of refilling the coffers. After all, whores, bartenders, and gamblers don't give charity.

Slowly the riders approached, and Gumbo cocked his pistol. Looking over at Walter he nodded, and put a red bandana over his nose and mouth.

Squinting through the underbrush he could see three men moving slowly down the road towards them. As they came within thirty feet he bolted from the brush and pulled up his pistol.

"Whoa there! Y'all come far 'nuf," he said, as the rest of his bunch swarmed out onto the road, weapons drawn.

"What in blue blazes?" Blake shouted angrily.

"Blue blazes is what you'll feel if you shout again, master Yank," Gumbo said coldly. "Get over there and relieve them fellas of their money," he said to Walter.

Walter spurred his horse and rode alongside Carrigan.

"Give me yer money," he commanded.

Carrigan hesitated for a moment then handed over his billfold.

"Given me that satchel there," Walter said pointing at the leather pouch of the deceased courier.

Carrigan removed the satchel and handed it to the man.

"You renegades," Blake blurted out. "You'll surely be hanged for this."

"Sure we will," Coffee Cup said then laughed.

Walter turned his horse around and came up to Baum. Baum eyed the five men coolly. Stopping short, Walter rifled through the satchel.

"Hey," he said in surprise. "There's a paper in here with your name on it, Gumbo!"

"Shut up," Gumbo shouted with such ferocity that everyone looked at him. "I oughta knock yer teeth out!"

The sound of a pistol shot rang out, and Billy cried, "I been shot!"

Pandemonium ensued. Billy spurred his horse into the woods, Coffee Cup fired at the Yankees, Gumbo's horse bolted down the road, Walter fired his pistol at the soldiers, and Jack chased after

Gumbo.

Blake lay back in the saddle, his revolver still smoking. He fired at the robbers as they fled. The closest brigand's horse bolted down the road.

Baum reached out and grabbed the satchel causing the rider to tip to the side and abandon his grip on the pouch. The contents spilled into the muddy road. Carrigan frantically tried to get his pistol free of its holster as a bullet whistled by his ear.

Terror filled him, as he got the weapon clear and fired at the man trying to kill him. Then, the robbers were gone; having fled into the woods.

"Quickly, LeRoy, Baum, back to the town," Blake shouted as he turned his horse and made a dash back down the road.

Carrigan jumped from his horse and scooped up the fallen items from the leather pouch. He shoved the muddy items into his coat and mounted the worried mare. Spurring the beast, he followed Baum and Blake back towards town.

CHAPTER 9

The town marshal seemed uninterested in Blake's description of the event. He was an older man with a full white mustache that hung down below his chin.

His face was wrinkled, and his eyes squinted at them as Blake pointed at his own uniform.

"We're officers with the Union, and this happened just a mile or so outside your town!"

"Not my jurisdiction, fellas!" the man said as he walked towards the tavern. "You'll have to bring this up to the sheriff, or to your commander. Aren't you boys typically manning the roads around here anyway?"

"Obviously not today," Baum said angrily. "Whoever they were, one's name was… Gumbo."

"Gumbo is a fella that's been around these parts lately. Yer first to complain about him. If you see him, come get me, I'll have a talk with 'em. Until then, I'm having a drink at the tavern. "Come inside if you boys would like to join me."

The Marshal opened the door to the tavern and

stepped inside.

"Seems he's not interested in our plight," Carrigan declared.

"Do you know what we should do?" Blake asked while looking down the street at the large white church.

"We should take a look around and see if that Gumbo fellow is in town and hand him over to the authorities."

"He's got friends. Not such a good idea," Baum reminded him.

Blake took a puff from his pipe.

"Good point."

"Wouldn't we be safer back at the hospital?" Carrigan asked. "Perhaps we should alert the General's staff about this plot to kidnap Captain Lincoln."

"Maybe. But, if the South is near surrender, Grant's surely got his hands full right now and probably so does his staff. The note says that they want him delivered to Goose Creek Bridge," Baum mused.

"Midnight on April fifth," Carrigan added.

"We should notify Colonel Geary and present him the letter. He can get a telegraph through to City Point," Blake decided. "Give me the letter and I'll present it to Geary as soon as we get back."

Baum held up the empty satchel.

"Empty as the head of a Senator," he stated.

"The contents fell out as they fled," Carrigan said as he reached inside his coat. "But, I grabbed up the letters off the ground before I followed you back to town."

"By damn boy, yer a credit to your uniform,"

Blake declared.

Carrigan produced a folded paper and handed it to Blake. "Here, take it."

Blake took the letter and opened it. "This isn't it," he said.

Carrigan went pale.

"What?"

"Maybe you missed it. Could it have been trampled into the mud?" Blake asked.

"I don't remember… the shooting… we all were trying to not get shot. The items fell into the mud, and I grabbed what was down there."

Blake took a draw from his pipe and exhaled.

"There were no other papers?"

"They may still have the coded letter," Carrigan suggested.

"Then sure as peach pie is good with coffee, they'll be on their way to get 'em," Baum exclaimed.

"Damn hellfire and brimstone," Blake cursed. "We're not in danger then, but the captain is!"

"Then let's get back to camp and tell someone," Baum advised.

"Check your pistols for spent empty chambers, we may need them on our ride," Blake said.

"Back to camp?" Baum asked.

"No, to Geary's command out at Old Farmwell."

"Then let's make haste," Carrigan stated while taking out his revolver, replacing his used caps, and refilling the chambers with a ball and powder.

Un-tethering his horse from the hitching post he mounted his steed. Baum and Blake were already in the saddle, and Blake motioned for them to move forward.

"Keep an eagle's eye out for any trouble," he

added as he took the lead.

* * *

Gumbo stopped his horse. He turned to the rest of his disorganized rabble, his face a mask of red fury. "As God is my witness, you bungling jugheads is gonna get us all hanged!"

He glared at Walter. "Damn it, Walter, where's that satchel?"

Walter looked sheepish as he held up a crumpled paper.

"This is all I saved, Gumbo."

He goaded his horse forward and handed Gumbo the paper.

"You're all as useless as tits on a boar," Gumbo scolded as he snatched the paper from Walter.

"Gumbo?" Billy said while doubled over in the saddle. "I think I need a doctor."

"He's been gut shot," Jack said as he rode up alongside Billy, then turned to face Gumbo.

"Bad?" Gumbo asked.

Jack didn't respond but shook his head.

"What you want to do now?"

Gumbo looked at the assembled men. Slowly he realized that he was holding the paper. Opening it, he looked it over.

It only took him a minute to read the note. A broad smile grew across his face. He glanced up to see the men looking confused at him.

"What is it?" Coffee Cup demanded.

"It's what we've been waiting for, fellas."

Gumbo chuckled.

"Gumbo..." Billy said, as he slipped from his saddle and fell onto the muddy forest floor. Leaves clung to his body as he rolled over, both hands clenching his wound. "You fellas meet me at Prichard's barn in an hour. I'll be along shortly."

Gumbo dismounted and slowly walked over towards Billy.

"What ya going to do, Gumbo?" Walter asked.

"Gonna get Billy here to a doctor. Best that it's only me doing it. You know what I mean?"

Walter smiled. "Oh, okay, Gumbo. You da boss."

"Now get!"

Gumbo knelt down to Billy.

Coffee Cup reached out and grabbed Walter's reins stopping the man before he got too far.

"That boy's gut shot. He's as good as dead, and Gumbo knows it."

"What you saying Coffee Cup?"

Walter looked befuddled.

"He's gonna ease that boy's way to hell," Coffee Cup said with a laugh. "Just thought you should know he's doing him a favor."

Walter looked shocked and horrified.

"He's gonna kill em?"

"Just remember that he's doing that boy a favor," Coffee Cup assured him.

"Now, come on and let's get to the Prichard's farm."

The three men rode into the forest.

Gumbo listened as the horse's hooves faded. He waited while Billy groaned with the pain of his wound.

"Them Yanks did you good, Billy," Gumbo said.

"You aint gonna get me a doctor, are ya?" Billy asked.

"No, I aint. But I'll ease your suffering, boy,"

Gumbo stood up and took down the canteen from Billy's saddle.

"I need a drink Gumbo, I need a drink real bad," Billy said, as he closed his eyes with the pain. "My mouth is dry as a bone... I'm so thirsty..." He started to convulse.

Gumbo pulled the cork from the canteen and lifted Billy up so he could drink from the lip. The boy took two long sips and stopped.

"How's that?" Gumbo asked.

"Good, Gumbo, real good."

Billy looked as if he was drifting off to sleep.

Gumbo removed his Arkansas toothpick and made two quick thrusts into Billy's chest over his heart.

The boy went rigid, and then his body became limp. Wiping the knife on the boy's shirt, Gumbo stood and re-corked the canteen. Placing it back on the saddle, he took up the horse's reins. Walking over to his horse Gumbo casually looked back at the lifeless body of Billy Preston.

"Sorry, boy, but business is business, and you was already a dead man," he said. "I'll see you soon, and we can both bark at Old Nick."

Climbing into the saddle, he steered his horse in the direction of Prichard's barn. He took in a deep breath of air and spurred his horse.

"I hope the devil doesn't know you're there for another hour or so, Bill."

He left Billy's corpse behind to be forgotten.

* * *

Colonel Geary put a cigar into his mouth as he looked out into the back yard of the two-story mansion home his command was occupying.

He was older than Blake, and his full black beard had hints of gray dispersed among the coarse strands of hair. His reputation was of a man who did not take to foolishness, and he had in the past, men put in the stockade for such behavior.

"You, all three, smell of liquor," Geary stated while turning to face the three men, "and horse."

"But, sir," Blake began. "These men not only tried to rob us, but they're neck deep in a plot to abduct Captain Lincoln."

"The President's son," Baum added.

"I know who the hell Captain Lincoln is, and so does everyone else. Damn it, do you understand that we're on the brink of winning this war?"

"Yes, sir," Blake answered.

"And you come to me with stories of Confederates planning to steal our Captain Lincoln, and you have no evidence to support it?"

"Sir, you have the word of three of your officers," Baum began.

"Officers who are stinking of whisky and clearly wallpapered." Geary drove home his point like a ramrod.

"At least send a telegram to Washington warning the President and the captain of the possible plot," Carrigan suggested.

"The lines are down," Geary said, as he took several long puffs while turning and staring out the window again.

"The rebel Forty Third Battalion is on a tear. Mosby's goddamn men are causing problems all over," he cursed angrily.

"A damn nuisance if you ask me. Sorry, but the lines are down for now. We could send a messenger, but like I said, Mosby's raiders are riding like Banshees all over these woods, doing their worst to harass us to no end. I'd hate to send one of our messengers to his death on a lark."

"We could go, sir," Carrigan suggested.

"All three of you?" Geary rolled his eyes. "Why don't you sober up before you suggest such an action that could get you killed."

Geary exhaled a long chimney of dark acrid smoke into the room.

"No time, sir." Blake cut in. "They mean to have the captain in their hands by April fifth, sir."

"Two days away," Geary said.

For a moment he paced back and forth in front of the window.

"Quite a pickle indeed."

Sitting down at his wide desk, he pulled out a piece of paper and dipped his ink pen into the well and scrawled quickly. He signed his name to the bottom of the note and stood up. Handing the paper to Blake he shook his head with exasperation.

"This is a release from your current duties and it details that you're to be given any help necessary to put an end to this plot against the Captain and the President. My advice is that you find a working telegraph and get your warning to the White House post haste."

"Yes, sir," Blake said, as he read the note and then folded it and put it in the black leather case secured to his belt.

"Better safe than sorry," Geary added while eying the three men with what appeared to be some suspicion.

He then relaxed his gaze and took another draw

on his cigar. "Now get the hell out of here and report back – provided Mosby's bastards don't get you first."

"Yes, sir!" Blake said feeling both relieved that they were not going to be court marshaled and trepidation regarding Mosby's marauders lurking close by.

CHAPTER 10

The barn was large, old, and covered in faded red paint. The wood was rough cut, knotty, and rotted in places. Along one side several square windows were cut.

Through one widow a neglected field could be seen; the grass was tall and waving in the breeze. In the distance, more than a hundred yards away, was the tree line.

The other window was covered by a pair of shutters that were nailed shut. The roof sagged in the middle making it appear as if it could slide off the top at any moment. The double doors to the structure were in as bad a shape; weathered wood frayed and gray, and one side falling half off its hinges. As Gumbo got closer, he could see through the spaces between the wall boards and see the light on the other side.

He chuckled. "You could throw a cat through the east wall and never hit wood." He slowly rode up to the front and waited for one of his men to call out to him.

"It's us, Gumbo," Walter shouted.

Climbing off his horse, Gumbo took up the reins and walked towards the main double doors. He tied up his steed under the eaves, pulled on the door to open it, and went inside.

"How long we gonna be here, Gumbo?" asked Jack.

"Not long. We got money to make, and time's not on our side," Gumbo said as he led his horse into the barn.

"So, what's the job?" Coffee Cup asked as he slipped his large hunting knife back into its sheath.

"We've been living high on the hog for the past few weeks. That money was fronted to us by some of Mosby's men, them gray-coats we met 'bout a month back."

"They had a job they wanted done, and I talked them into lettin' us do it. We was just waiting on that layabout Terrence to get the information and bring it to us. Son of a bitch if he didn't somehow let then blue-bellies get his satchel and almost cost us nearly a hundred dollar apiece!"

Walter looked concerned. "Where do ya think he's at now?"

"He's probably hiding in Alexandria by now, afraid to show his face for his incompetence or treachery...I'm not sure which. Either way, them fellas we tried to rob, they had his bag, and in it a note from old Mosby. Looks like we'll be getting our chink."

"Now how much we getting? I mean since Billy and Terrence are no longer going to get paid?" Jack asked.

"We'll figure that out later. Just know that we're

going to earn that money. This aint no gettin' a slave that run off the farm job. This is armed men looking for a fight kinda job," Gumbo made clear.

"You're running your gums like a granny. Just tell us what the job is," Coffee Cup demanded as he flexed his fists in frustration.

"Okay, the job is to steal them Federal's President's son."

"Are you out of your mind?" Jack shook his head. "I hear that boy's got a contingent of soldiers around him at all times."

"Ya, I heard that boy is held up tight as a drum at City Point. We aint gonna get into City Point," Coffee Cup said with a dismissive laugh.

"You boys are thick as ditches." Gumbo shook his head. "We aint gonna get him down at City Point. He's taking a little trip with his daddy to Washington, and coming back through Alexandria, Manassas, Gaines, and then south down to City Point."

"He'll probably be traveling with an escort, but not many men I think, maybe four or five."

"How in hell do you know this?" Jack challenged.

"I been working this out since I talked to Mosby's boys. Now, they sent a message. It's time and the man we want is coming through Gaines on the train," Gumbo stated.

"Why they want him?" Walter asked his face betraying no understanding whatsoever.

"Who cares?" Coffee Cup blurted. "Them fellas paying us good to get him, and that's good enough for me."

"We got a deliver him to Goose Creek Bridge by April fifth," Gumbo added.

"Goose Creek?" Coffee Cup laughed. "There's

thousands of blue-bellies between us and there."

Jack leaned back against a broken stable board,

"We'll need to grab him early and make our way off the roads. It'll be slow going, but we could go cross-country through the Fairfax to the Waterfall. From there it's just a snap to Goose Creek Bridge," he said.

"Then shut up ,and let's have a look at this map," Gumbo chided as he pulled out a folded map of Fairfax and Loudoun Counties. Unfolding it, he laid it over several flat boards that looked like a workbench.

*   *   *

Baum unrolled a map of the surrounding counties. He ran his finger along the Alexandria road from Washington D.C. to Middleburg.

"So, he's taking the train part or all of the way. Makes sense, the train is the only secure path I figure; moves fast and is loaded with troops."

Baum scoured the map.

"Here's the railroad that Captain Lincoln will most likely take coming from D.C. and heading down to City Point. If I were intending to abduct a Federal Army officer and transport him to Goose Creek Bridge," he moved his finger to the location of the bridge, "where would I do it?"

Blake looked over the map for a moment. "I agree, somewhere around Alexandria is the best bet. Troop counts are low there since most of the fighting is south and the area has been secure for a year or more. Then I'd travel straight to Goose Creek off the roads."

"I agree," Carrigan added. "But the closest distance between Goose Creek and the railroad is a straight line."

He drew his finger across the map between the two points.

"Devereux Station," he said.

"But we have one big problem," Blake stated.

"What's that?" Baum looked concerned.

"Between here," Blake pointed at Devereux Station, "and there," he pointed at Goose Creek, "are Mosby's raiders trotting about."

"All we have to do is to get to Manassas and send a telegram," Baum said.

"What if the telegraph is out there too?" Carrigan asked while lighting his pipe.

"Then we'll need to press on to Devereux Station, or all the way to Alexandria if we have to," Blake said.

"We're wasting daylight, we'd better be on our way," Baum said.

He refolded his map and put it inside his coat.

"We need to make it to Manassas as soon as possible."

"Agreed," Blake said. "Let's be at it!"

The rain fell in buckets. A fresh smell of grass, trees and mud filled the air. After a while the rain stopped and the sun came out.

As late afternoon came, the road was drying out, and Carrigan watched the small puddles of mud dwindling. Looking to his left and right, he could see the country farms that bordered the road as he passed them; small colloquial homes, the types that Alexis De Tocqueville had written about years earlier.

He noted that at one farm the houses appeared ravaged by the war, abandoned, or grossly neglected. A mile down the road another farm house appeared well-maintained and recently painted. The contrasts of war were ever present.

"Watch your left," Blake said from the front.

Folding back the flap on his holster he put his hand on his pistol. The approaching group of people appeared to be locals— two men on horseback with rifles draped over their laps, two women riding a buckboard, and several children scurrying from side to side.

The men were young, maybe twenty and twenty five respectively, and the women, perhaps sixteen and nineteen. One of the men slowed his horse and looked at them from under a wide-brimmed slouch hat.

"Where you all coming from?" he asked.

"Middelburg," Baum replied.

"Any you fellas hear 'bout raiders up in them parts?"

"Some," Blake answered. "Why do you ask?"

"We's coming from Oatlett way south, and them raiders done killed my pa, ma, and two sisters. Them bastards done burned our farm and took our cattle. Me and my brother, little Joe, we're on our way back from Cherry Hill with our wives when we discovered the killings. Done buried the family nigh on three days ago. We just don't want to run into them raiders, sir, that's why I'm asking."

"Some raiding going on in the area, you keep an eye out," Baum said.

The man touched the brim of his hat.

"Much obliged to you, sir, fer your kindness. God watch over you," he said as he motioned with his head to his family.

"Let's get a move on, it'll be dark soon enough and we better be in town before it settles."

Blake held up his hand, and without a word motioned them forward. They began moving again southeast towards Manassas.

The air was warm as the sun began its fall towards the west. An incessant cacophony of bird sounds emanated from the forest.

The town of Gaines was only a few more miles ahead, and Carrigan was getting fatigued.

"I sure hope that they have the telegraph working in Gaines," he said.

"I just hope they have a tavern and maybe a nice hotel that's open," Blake called back. "Baum, what do you think?"

"Whisky and a fine meal sound like heaven to me!" Baum laughed.

Ahead a column of Federal soldiers appeared as they moved in lockstep down the road. At the front, Carrigan saw a young Lieutenant, a thin blonde mustache and goatee adorning his face.

He led what appeared to be fresh troops, each of the soldiers armed with Spencer rifles. Holding his hand up, he halted the column.

"Hoo," he shouted to his subordinates. "Good day, gentlemen," he said as his soldiers stopped.

"Good day to you." Blake halted. "Coming from Manassas?"

"With fresh troops. We've been ordered to reinforce Colonel Geary's forces and help stomp out Mosby's renegades in the area."

"Is the telegraph working in Manassas?" Blake asked.

"When we were there today it was working fine. I got my marching orders from Washington directly," the young officer stated. "We're hoping to make it to

Haymarket by tonight."

"How about Gaines? Telegraph working there?" Baum asked.

"Couldn't tell you, we didn't stop to use the telegraph there," the young man said.

"Good luck to you, Lieutenant," Blake said as he began riding forward.

"To you too, sir," the Lieutenant said as he did a quick salute, then motioned his column forward.

Carrigan watched as the new troops, some young and some quite old, marched past on their way northwest. It felt strange to see these men, their short-barrel repeating rifles over their shoulders, well-fitting uniforms and new shoes.

A far cry from the motley men torn to pieces on his operating table. Those men were beat, tired, and thin from hunger. They wore ill fitted uniforms, and mismatched shoes that tore at their un-stocking feet, and they were grim and weary folk, terrified shells of humanity.

Baum, Blake, and Carrigan moved past the soldiers, leaving the long column of blue behind. The road was fairly straight, and Carrigan could see the signpost at the crossroad that read, Gaines - 5 miles.

The horses were getting tired and the excitement of the morning finally settled on him with full force.

"I'll be glad to put my head down on a pillow tonight," Carrigan said.

"I'll be glad to get some strong rye whisky into my stomach along with a steak or two," Blake confessed.

"We're not there yet my compatriots," Baum stated with a nod. Rebels could spoil any hope of a decent night's sleep or meal at any moment."

"I'm sure they wouldn't begrudge us at least one

decent night of sleeping. I'm damn well tired of sleeping on a cot I'll tell you!" Blake said while rubbing his lower back.

As they approached the town of Gaines, Carrigan saw the remnants of breastworks and trenches crisscrossing the light woods on either side of the road. Through the trees, a colorful meadow was visible.

Some children, between the ages of eight and twelve dashed out onto the road. One blonde haired boy held a wooden pistol at arm's length pointing it at an older raven-haired boy who carried a long stick.

"You'll surrender, or we'll hunt down your soldiers and put them in the stockade," the blonde shouted.

"You is at my mercy... Lee, me and my Federals have you outnumbered." The dark haired boy slashed at the other with the branch.

"You'll not have me ,Grant," yelled the blonde haired boy.

"Then you is gonna die," the black haired boy said.

Three other children appeared on the road, and they rushed the blonde who dropped his wooden pistol and covered his face as all the boys piled on top of him. A fight erupted and two boys rolled around on the moist muddy road in front of Blake, Baum and Carrigan.

"I'll knock you down," the blonde shouted as the older boy rolled on top of him and was about to deliver a punch to his face.

Blake shouted. "That's enough!"

All the boys stopped and looked over, just now realizing that they were not alone. The older boy with black hair climbed to his feet.

The blonde stood up beside him. Both dusted off

their clothes and looked up.

"You Federals?" the dark haired boy asked.

"We are," Baum answered. "How far to Gaines?"

"Just down the road, mister," the blonde said while pointing.

"Now, which one of you is Lee?" Blake asked looking very stern.

"Uh, sir it was me. They always make me and my friends Lee's troops," the blonde said. "I like Lee—he's got a big beard, like my pa!"

"Don't pay him no mind, we trade off sometimes. And today we is beating back Lee's army," the older boy said.

"Very well, carry on boys, but you'd better clean up that scrape on your face or it'll get infected," Blake added as he spurred his horse and moved forward, parting the group of boys in half.

Carrigan passed the group just as a mob of young boys rushed from the opposite side of the road. The blonde boy shouted.

"Don't take any prisoners…we got 'em on the run now!"

Carrigan looked back over his shoulder to see the boys turn and dash back towards the abandon trenches.

"Retreat!" shouted the dark haired boy as he disappeared into the woods. The road was again empty.

Blake mused, "Tides of war are fickle!"
"They don't know how real their playing is to the battles that took place here," Carrigan said solemnly. "At least they'll keep their arms and legs when going home tonight."

CHAPTER 11

The men rode in silence as Gumbo led the way. Coffee Cup held the reins in his left hand and kept his right hand resting on the handle of his pistol. Walter rode behind and he removed his Bowler and wiped his brow with a white handkerchief. Jack kept rear guard, as he balanced his rifle across his lap.

The weather was clear and the mud had almost dried with the gentle breeze that wafted across the meadows. In the distance, Gumbo could see gullies and small stands of hickory and birch trees. In the air hung a sweet smell, like a mother's kitchen in summer, filled with the scent of peach pies and apple dumplings. Gumbo drank in the scent, all the while scanning the horizon for Federals, or worse—other brigands.

"We're gettin' close to Gaines," Jack said. "Another hour or so."

Gumbo remained silent, his eyes scanning the foreground for any movement.

"Watch that there grove, Coffee Cup," he

73

commanded.

Coffee Cup reached down to his side and pulled up a spyglass. Extending it, he searched the trees.

A boy stumbled out and came quickly running. Behind him was a group of kids, some throwing rocks and others holding up sticks.

"Some boys, Gumbo, no Federals," he said as he kept watching the area.

"Them boys sure know how to play," he added.

"Maybe we should go help him," Walter ventured.

"Watlter, you is as dumb as a carpetbagger," Jack scolded. "After they see us them boys will go off and tell their daddies that some men come riding through here." He shook his head. "And where do you think them daddies are going to as soon as they know there's four strangers riding through?"

"Now what's happening?" Walter asked Coffee Cup.

"Two groups of boys, and they're fighting up a storm." Coffee Cup laughed. "Wait – now they're scattering, going back into the woods."

"Keep moving," Gumbo quietly said.

Slowly they entered the woods. They maneuvered between the birch trees, their horses hooves smashing down the rotted leaves.

The smell was rich, and Gumbo delighted in drawing in the aroma of the woods. It reminded him of when he was a boy, hiding in the thick mangroves of the Louisiana swamps.

He'd been living in a two-room shack with his daddy and mother and three older brothers near Baton Rouge. His daddy would take the family horse and go into town to gamble, which is how he supported the family.

Unfortunately, the man was less lucky than he was smart and often times came home drunk with just the clothes on his back. When he was in a drunken state of mind he would beat all those he could get his hands on.

Gumbo would lay awake at night, listening for the clopping of hooves, and then as he heard his father swearing at the horse for making him fall to the ground, Gumbo would slip out the window and run into the forest.

There he would hide, waiting for dawn. One morning he returned to find all gone. They had up and left him all alone.

Looking down, Gumbo saw the ground was strange. Though covered in rotted leaves it seemed to vibrate with each step, radiating out like ripples on a lake.

The horse stumbled churning up the ground, and a clump of bones came up.

"What the hell?" he said as he stopped his horse.

"It's a graveyard!" Walter said in a panic.

Getting down from his horse, Gumbo cleared away some of the detritus. Everywhere laid crumpled clothes, uniforms, shoes, rifle butts, and bones... all covered in leaves.

Kicking away some of the leaves he stirred up a skull, the front of the face smashed in by some forgotten force.

"You're right, Walter – this here is a graveyard, but all are lost souls," Gumbo said as if he was lost in deep thought. "Forgotten souls," he restated as he climbed back up onto his horse.

"Plum forgotten by man, but buried by God," Jack said with reverence.

They rode for some time, silent with their thoughts. Gumbo maintained the lead and the forest took on an eerie feel as every once in a while the horses would churn up a head, an arm, or stumble over a rusted weapon.

After nearly an hour the ground changed and the horses had solid footing again. In the air was a hint of smoke, and in the distance Gumbo heard the sound of a blacksmith leveling his hammer on iron.

A flash of blue halted Gumbo and he raised his hand to signal the rest of his men to stop. They waited a few moments while they listened. Ahead he saw the edge of a fence.

Waving in the wind was a blue blanket, hung out to dry on a clothesline. His heart slowly returned to a normal pattern of beating, and he motioned his men forward.

Emerging from the tree line they were on the outskirts of Gaines. A two story home, surrounded with a perimeter fence of wooden slats was in front of them and he steered his men around it and into a small alleyway that led to the streets of Gaines.

The sky was darkening as the sun set in the west. A brilliant pink and purple hue came over the town.

Gumbo entered the first tavern he came too and purchased a bottle of whisky. Coffee Cup, Jack and Walter sat at a table near the back of the room.

A few Federal soldiers were at the bar, but they were clearly green, young men more interested in a few drinks than shooting southerners.

"Gumbo?" Walter asked as he picked up his glass and helped himself to the bottle of whisky.

"What's bothering you?" Gumbo snapped.

"Them fellas we rode over today, the dead

ones…"

Walter trailed off as he looked over both shoulders.

"You don't think that they're mad at us for ridin' on top of 'em, do ya?"

Gumbo looked at Jack and Coffee Cup, then turned his attention to Walter.

"Walter, them fellas are dead, and if you had the choice to stay here in Virginia or go on to paradise, what would you chose? I don't think them fellas given a goddamn pile of pig shit that some bastard was standing on top of 'em."

Coffee Cup dribbled some of the whisky down his chin. "You, Gumbo," he choked, "is the devil's own! You is a devil." He laughed loudly.

Jack sat quietly, as if he was not even at the same table. Slowly he tipped up his glass and drank down the contents. Putting it down he refilled it again, then looked over at Walter and spoke.

"I'd care, Walter… I'd care a lot."

Walter looked at his glass with a frown. Taking the whisky bottle he poured the glass half full, much more than any of his comrades.

Drinking it down in one draft, he closed his eyes tightly and folded his hands on the table.

"God, here my prayer, deliver me into your arms when my time comes, and let me not know that there is anyone traipsing across the top of my last resting place!"

Coffee Cup leaned over and smiled broadly.

"He aint listening to you, boy. He's troubled with all them fellas who's dying right now at the hands of this war. So, why don't you be a man and just drown those thoughts in more whisky?"

CHAPTER 12

Gaines bustled with people. The night was dark, no moon was present, and Carrigan waited patiently with Blake and Baum for a table in the dining room of the local inn.

"It was lucky that we got the rooms here… the town seems rather filled to capacity," Carrigan commented.

A young blonde haired woman in a yellow and white dress scuttled by with her arms laden with plates of food. The smell of the food filled his nostrils as she went by, and his stomach growled loudly.

"Good lord!" Blake laughed. "Sounds like you have a bear loose behind your belt!"

Baum chuckled, then peered into the dining room.

"They're clearing a table. We should be in soon."

This way, gentlemen," said a large man with a dark black goatee and mustache. "We appreciate you Federals around here keeping the riff-raff out."

"Glad we could be of service," Carrigan said.

The man stopped and glanced over his shoulder at

Carrigan.

"You from Boston?"

"No, England," Carrigan stated.

"England?" The man started to walk again. "Long way from home, aren't you?"

"A man's destiny is not always fulfilled on the threshold of his own home," Carrigan said.

"Well put," the man said, as he came to a linen covered table in the back of the room. "Do let me know if you're not pleased with the meal or service." He turned on his heels and headed back out the door into the hall.

"Strange how he asked you about Boston," Blake said.

"Seemed good that you answered with England instead," Baum smiled.

"You colonists have very strange customs." Carrigan shook his head.

"Good evening, gentlemen."

A young man came up to their table; he held a set of menus in one arm, with a white towel hanging off the other.

"This is quite the cosmopolitan town," Baum added.

"The war's swelled our population here, sir. With the soldiers came the new businesses," the young man explained as he handed the menus to them. "Now, can I interest you in some refreshments?"

Blake's eyes sparkled. "Of course. Bring us a bucket of beer, and a bottle of your good whisky," He winked at the man. "You get me? The good stuff."

The young man smiled. "I get your meaning, sir. I'll see to it."

Turning back to his company, Blake shook his

head in frustration.

"Pretty shame that the wire is down here."

"Damn shame indeed," Carrigan replied. "And the next Telegraph is all the way in Manassas."

"It'll be at least noon before we can send the message to the Whitehouse," Baum added just as the waiter returned.

"Your beer, gentlemen. I'll have your whisky in just a moment."

The young man turned and headed back out of the room.

"So what do you think these villains are up to?" Baum asked.

Blake lit a match and ignited the tobacco in his pipe.

"No good, I'm sure. But where is more the question."

Carrigan poured some beer into his glass and handed the bucket to Blake.

"I believe that the important question gentlemen, is not only where, but when. We know that they must have their prey delivered alive to Goose Creek Bridge by April fifth, and that gives them two days to do it."

"Ah, yes, I see what you're saying. If they have two days left, then we must assume that they will be at their ambush point sometime tomorrow."

"The day time is too risky for a small band to act with due diligence, ergo they will need to take the captain early in the morning or around dusk."

Baum removed a map of the county from his leather satchel. Then he removed a soft measuring tape and a divider.

Clearing away the plates and tableware he laid out the map on the table. For a moment he was deep in thought, then unrolled his measuring tape and set his divider to a certain set of inch marks.

"That is how far we can travel in any day at a casual pace. Not counting stopping to relieve ourselves, or to talk to someone. We must assume that during the daylight our counterparts are traveling casually off the road as not to be spotted by Federal patrols, which means that they would be a little slower than this measure indicates. So what do you think? Less by a mile an hour?"

"Sounds reasonable," Blake said, as he placed a full glass of beer in front of Baum.

"Now if we make some adjustments, we get this span of distance." He held up the divider with a knowing wink. "Understand that there is quite a lot of error that can figure into this. But, if we assume that they left about the same time as we did..."

He stopped and laid out his tape in a straight line to Manassas from Middleberg.

"There, a nice reference line," he stated.

Carrigan watched as Baum put his divider down at Middleberg on a straight line. Moving the divider in a half-arc he declared, "Our quarry is somewhere within, plus or minus a mile or two of this curve, my friends."

"Plus or minus a mile along this curve?" Blake looked annoyed.

"Yes." Baum said with a wide smile while taking out his pipe and stuffing it full of tobacco.

Carrigan reached across the table and put his finger down on a point on the map.

"They could be here then!"

Lifting his finger Carrigan revealed Gaines. Baum held up a lit match and looked smug. Putting the match into the bowl of his pipe he took several long puffs, exhaling the smoke over the table.

"Yes," he simply said.

"Surely you don't think that they would be dumb enough to stay in Gaines? Especially after their little fiasco with us, do you?" Carrigan asked, his eyebrows a bit knitted.

"One, they don't know that we know. Two, they did not seem the most thoughtful characters God created, and three, they are in a hurry – pressed for time as it were. We all know what happens when one is in a hurry—they make mistakes. They're probably here somewhere."

"Do you think we should make a few discrete inquiries?" Carrigan asked.

"Who should we ask? Perhaps our waiter might know," Blake suggested.

As if on cue, the young man arrived with a bottle of Clinchfield whisky and four glasses.

"Have you decided on a supper, gentlemen?" He looked down at the map on the table.

"Yes, I'll have the jack rabbit stew, cornbread, and sweet potatoes," Blake said.

"I'll have your beef steak, yellow potatoes, and bread," Carrigan stated.

"Do you have the trout tonight?" Baum asked.

"We do, sir. Caught 'em this week and we keep 'em in a tub out back – as fresh as if you caught it yourself this day," the young man declared.

"Then I'll have your trout pan roasted, yellow potatoes, and your greens," Baum said.

"Also, we were wondering if there might be someone here in town who might have a watchful eye and be interested in earning a silver dollar?"

The young man smiled softly.

"Again, gentlemen, I get your meaning and if you have any questions, I can help you."

"Any strangers come to town…three or four riding together, and one may be injured?" Blake asked.

"I've not seen any injured men come to town, other than soldiers, sir. We get lots of travelers coming and going since the war began. But if you're interested, I might make some inquiries."

"Discreet, I trust," Carrigan said.

"That means—" Blake began but was cut off.

"I know what that means, sir, I'm quite well educated. The war's just interrupted my life and working here pays my rent until I can travel to San Francisco in California," he said.

"What's your education in?" Baum asked.

"The law, gentlemen, the law," he smiled broadly. "Now, I'll see what I can do to earn that silver dollar from you."

He turned and left the table.

"That was most unexpected," Blake said.

"Indeed," Carrigan replied. "Must be difficult being forced to work as a waiter in this burg rather than practicing law."

"I would bet on it," Baum said.

"Without a doubt," Blake added as he tilted up his glass of beer and finished it in one draft.

"If they're somewhere along this arch," Carrigan said pointing again at the map. "Where do you think they will be by tomorrow?"

Baum looked thoughtful again.

"Well, if we consider that it took us half a day to get here from Geary's headquarters, we could safely assume…" He adjusted his dividers again. "Somewhere along this curve."

He made a half-arc tangent away from the town of Gaines. This time the arc showed a point just outside Manassas.

"We must assume that Captain Lincoln will be traveling forty miles an hour, so our eager villains will most likely be at an ambush point somewhere along here." Baum pointed at the map. "The junction to Devereux Station is a likely spot, give or take a mile or two."

Blake poured some beer into his glass. "A mile or two is a lot of distance to cover, especially when we're talking about the area and not just a linear distance."

Carrigan sat back in his chair, his hands clasped together as if in prayer. "It seems to me they must remain hidden near the railroad. Easiest to abduct him from a stationary train rather than a moving one."

"Bravo," Baum said with a laugh. "Indeed it is."

Blake rolled his eyes. "There is just three of us to do all this task."

"Then what do you suggest, Mister Blake," Baum asked, irritated.

"We get to Manassas, and contact Devereux Station and notify them, then we send a telegraph to Barker's Station Just to the East of Devereux and ask them to keep Captain Lincoln there until the danger is abated."

"If only we knew that the wire in Manassas is working," Carrigan said. "If it isn't, we'll need to make our way toward Devereux Station, post haste." He leaned forward and poured his glass three fingers deep of whisky. "We'll need to maintain a contingent plan if we're blocked."

"We have the orders from Geary, and when we get to Manassas we can secure troops to help with the search around Devereux," Blake stated.

Carrigan stared into his glass for a moment, swirling the amber liquid.

"Damn impractical."

"What is?" Baum frowned.

"Two surgeons and a cartographer chasing brigands," Carrigan said while shaking his head.

"Need I remind you both that we are officers in the Federal Army – we are soldiers," Blake affirmed.

"Your dinners, gentlemen," the voice of the young waiter rang out.

Each man finished his meal quickly. The conversation was kept to a minimum while each stuffed food into their mouth.

Finally, Blake sat back, and polished off his latest glass of whisky.

"Gentlemen, if you will excuse me, I must visit the latrine," Blake said as he stood up and put his napkin on the table.

"He's just trying to skip out on paying the bill." Baum laughed.

"Just for that comment – I shall take extra-long," Blake stated as he turned and left the room.

Following the signs to the outhouse he walked down a long hallway to the back door and into a large enclosed backyard. At the very back was a tall single door outhouse.

Blake felt the heaviness of the liquor. Looking down he noted the simple stone pathway that led to the wood structure.

Placing his hand on the door handle he pulled, but the door was locked from within. Knocking on the door he heard a frustrated voice on the other side.

"I'll be out in a moment!"

Stepping back Blake fell off the stone path and wandered about in what appeared to be a lush and fruitful garden. Surely this was where some of the fresh ingredients, herbs, vegetables and fruits would have been harvested from.

He heard the wooden door slam against the frame and turned to look. A portly man stood in front of the structure, still cinching his belt.

"Damn this thing," the man swore. "Plum never buy pants without getting' suspenders," he said, then noticed Blake standing there.

"Sorry, Yankee, didn't see you there. It's all yours now."

Blake approached, but noticed the man staring at him. "Do I know you, sir?" Blake asked.

"Maybe we met somewhere before," the man said. "You ever been in the Angola prison before?"

Blake scoffed in disgust. "Good God, man, never!"

"Uh, just you seemed familiar and I don't remember where I'd seen you."

"When you remember, please do call upon me," Blake said sarcastically. "Until then excuse me –" He curtly stepped into the latrine, closed and latched the door. "Ignorant buffoon," he muttered.

CHAPTER 13

Walter slowly walked back to the tavern. He looked up at the shingle. In black letters it read 'Hite Tavern'.

What a funny name for a public house, he thought.

Taking a handkerchief from his pocket, he wiped his sweaty brow. His mind was filled with the effects of too much beer and he felt as though he knew the man at the outhouse. But from where?

He was not a lawman, a judge, or a slave owner. The man was a Federal soldier – a Yankee.

He was lost in thought as he opened the door. Stepped into the dimly lit room, he walked over to where Gumbo was sitting. Coffee Cup was sitting there too, a cigar in his mouth and a half bottle of whisky on the table.

"So, you mean to tell me that you were in the shitter all this time?" Coffee Cup asked loudly.

"What the hell took you so long?" Gumbo asked angrily. "You aint on your own time now, we're working."

"Uh, I couldn't find an open outhouse, so I had to go lookin'. I got chased out of the yard of the house down the street, and finally found me a place to sit around the next street. Some inn or something I think. Nicely sanded seat," he proudly declared.

"You is as dumb as an addle-minded idiot!" Coffee Cup chided. "What is that you do when yer riding out in the woods, do you look for a sanded seat to sit on?"

"No," Walter replied uncomfortably. "I'd just do my business in the woods."

"Plenty of woods around if there's no shitter to use," Coffee Cup said.

"Forget about that." Gumbo slid an empty glass to Walter. "Have a drink and let's talk about something else."

"Where's Jack?" Walter asked.

"He's enjoying the comforts of a fine belle of the ball at that bawdy house down the street. I suspect we aint gonna see him till the dawn's first light." Gumbo guffawed.

"I'll be glad when this is all done," Walter said while taking a drink from his glass. "What you gonna do with your share, Gumbo?"

"I'm gonna move out to the territories. I hear that there's lots of money to be made in whisky and guns," he said.

"You, Coffee Cup?" Walter asked.

"I think that I might just head on over to Chicago, I hear that there's plenty of fools willin' to part with hard earned coin there." Coffee Cup malevolently chuckled.

"What about you, Walter? You gonna open a dress shop?"

"I thought that I'd go to Texas, get me a real nice spread there. I'll raise me some cattle and maybe have a dog."

Coffee Cup boasted a mighty laugh.

"You dreaming about Texas! That Texas will swallow you up and spit out yer bones!"

Walter cast his eyes down to his glass. For a moment the table was quiet and he just swirled his whisky around.

Finally he brought up the glass and took a drink, and shrugged his shoulders. "I was just kidding, fellas. I'd just probably go with Gumbo to the Territories."

"Now, that's a good hound dog," Coffee Cup said with a broad grin.

"Shut up both of you," Gumbo chided. "We got to get out of here early, so why don't you two go over to that whore house and find Jack and tell him that we ride out of here at 4 a.m. If he aint ready, he's givin' up his share."

Coffee cup chuckled as he grabbed the whisky bottle and poured himself more.

"You sure are a mule skinning son of a bitch, Gumbo – you keep giving orders and I'll keep doing what ever in the hell I want to."

Walter stood up. "I'll go."

"Sure you will, Walt, and we can be sure that you'll be sitting in the parlor waiting for Jack like a good hound dog," Coffee Cup slighted.

Walter shrugged his shoulders.

"I'll go," he repeated.

Walter turned and walked out of the tavern. As he reached the outside stoop, he stopped to close the door. On the inside he heard Gumbo talking to Coffee Cup.

"He does make a good hound," Gumbo said, then laughed.

The night was clear and starry. Walter looked around at the houses and shops as he wandered towards the bawdy house at the end of town.

Gaines was a small town, only made bigger by the railroad and the invasion of the Federals. A lot of businesses sprang up and lots of folks with things to trade or sell filled it. New buildings were being constructed, and taverns and inns were filled to capacity.

He came to the end of an alley and looked down the main street. The smell of cooking meat filled the air as he passed one of the inns.

He could see the Red Tavern was bustling, the many hitching posts were surrounded by horses and patrons were even standing outside in the street, their glasses and mugs brimming with spirits and beer.

"Good evening," Walter said as he passed a group of Federals.

"Lovely evening indeed," one said to him as he passed.

Foot traffic was heavy at this end of town. Walter approached the bawdy house; the sign was painted bright red and pink.

"Virginia Bell's Salon," he read aloud.

He removed his hat and mopped the sweat from his head and neck with his handkerchief. Putting his hand on the door, he turned the knob and entered.

As he stepped into the room the smell of flowery perfume assailed his nostrils. A set of stairs rose up from just inside the entrance.

Walter could hear sounds echoing down from above; mostly unpleasant…

"Another gentleman?" a soft voice called from the hallway.

Coming into the entrance, a thin woman dressed in a petticoat and laced boots emerged. Over one bare shoulder she carried a pink parasol, and over the other she had a riding crop.

"Ladies," she called loudly. "We have a new gentleman to entertain!"

Filtering out of the two parlors a host of young, old, pretty, and homely women came. Walter was surrounded on all sides.

The madam gave a bawdy laugh and twirled her parasol. She approached him and smiled.

"Take your pick, good sir. We have the finest ladies in this burg!"

"Uh…I just come here to tell a friend of mine something," Walter stammered.

"Come now, my saucy friend…surely one of these girls tickles your fancy?"

Fidgeting with his hat, Walter struggled for his words. He had always felt uncomfortable around women and now that he was surrounded by them, he was near a state of panic.

His head started to sweat, and he removed his handkerchief again and mopped his brow.

"Thank you ma'am, but I just come here to tell my friend Jack—"

"That you, Walter?" shouted Jack from the left side parlor. "What in the hell are you doing here? Come to get a little touch?"

Jack laughed as he approached him.

"He's not keen on girls, but I'll take a few more," Jack said, as he made his way through the mob. He boomed a great belly laugh and pulled Walter over to a circular red parlor couch.

"Gumbo send you?"

"He did," Walter said feeling much relieved that he was no longer the center of attention. "He says that you better be ready to go at four in the morning or you're giving up your share."

Jack laughed again. "That Gumbo is quite a mouthy bastard. I think one of these days I'll put a bullet in his liver."

Walter smelled the thick vapor of brandy coming from Jack. It was as if he had bathed in the liquor.

The man was clearly drunk, but strangely lucid. He was the only man that Walter had ever known who was nice to him, and could drink copious amounts of liquor and still remain reasonably sober.

"You can go tell Gumbo that I'll be there when I'm done. "Now, I got some humping to do. If you ain't going to take a woman, at least take my brandy glass and finish 'er up for me."

Jack smiled while handing the glass to Walter. "It ain't cheap." He slapped Walter on the back once and grabbed a lovely red headed woman whom he clearly knew and made for the stairs.

Walter sat back as a dark haired young woman approached. She wore a white and yellow dress and no shoes and she appeared tired and maybe even a bit drunk.

She came over and sat next to him and put her arms around his shoulders. She looked at his face with a queer look, and fell unconscious in his arms.

He held still, fearing to wake her. The glass of brandy was trapped under her torso and he felt the urge to retrieve his handkerchief again – but knew it would be impossible.

The sweat trickled down his face and onto his shirt, and he looked down at the girl's dark curls and slumped body.

How could any girl want to sit next to me, even if she was paid to? he thought. I'm ugly, stupid and sweat all the time.

He felt the girl move slightly.

When she comes awake in a couple of hours she'll look at me with disgust and find another place to make a bed. Even that feller at the shitter could see I was a worthless crap heap, like Coffee Cup says… that feller at the shitter could see it – damn Yankee.

For a moment he was lost in thought.

That feller at the outhouse sure looked familiar. But who could he be?

Like a hammer between the eyes, Walter felt a sudden pain of remembrance.

That feller was one of the horseman who we tried to rob today!

Looking down at the girl again he felt like he wanted to push her off his lap, but then again he didn't want to wake her and get that look… the look of disgust. It was going to be a long night.

CHAPTER 14

Carrigan woke to the sound of someone knocking on his door.

"Who is it?"

"The damn chambermaid, who in blazes do you think it is?" Blake bellowed. "It's four in the morning and we better be off. Get yourself together and meet us down in the dining room for breakfast."

Carrigan heard Blake stomp back down the hall, and then the stairs. He lit a lamp and walked over to a small table in the corner of the room.

Quickly, he poured some water from the pitcher and washed his face and hands. He took out his shaving kit and lathered up his face. With each stroke, he slowly took off his whiskers.

When he'd finished, he tossed the dirty water out of the window, then replaced the basin. He got dressed and headed down stairs.

The aroma of biscuits, and bacon was unmistakable, and his stomach protested loudly as he headed into the dining room.

Blake and Baum were already seated, and a pot of coffee was steaming in the middle of the table. Baum had his pipe in his mouth and was blowing smoke rings across the table while Blake talked about the road to Manassas.

"Now we should be double careful from here on out," Blake said as Carrigan sat. "We wouldn't want our limey friend to end up buried here in the States would we?" He laughed.

"Buried? Here in the Colonies, most distasteful," Carrigan joked. "Notwithstanding my own concern for my skin, we sure wouldn't want those rakes to do something rash."

Baum shifted in his chair and picked up his coffee cup. Taking a sip he replaced it on the table and pointed with the stem of his pipe at the salt shaker.

"This is Gaines here, and Manassas here." Baum pointed at his coffee cup. "A distance of ten miles. The road is regularly patrolled. I was there not more than a month ago, and they have a federally appointed marshal and constable. The likelihood of us having any trouble on the way to Manassas is pretty slim. We should be there by six at the latest. Plenty of time to eat breakfast, ride there, find the telegraph, and send our message."

"So you have it all figured out, eh cartographer?" Blake asked as he lifted his coffee cup to his mouth, blew the steam from the top, and took a drink. "But you've not accounted for fate," he said confidently.

Carrigan reached for the coffee pot and poured some of the hot liquid into the thick white porcelain cup in front of him. Hoisting the cup to his mouth he took a sip of the bitter liquid.

Baum looked incredulous.

"You, a surgeon, telling me, a cartographer, to consider the mumbo-jumbo of fate? I gave you more credit than that old man." He laughed.

"Good God," Blake boasted. "You're a numbers man if ever I've seen one. Well, let me tell you something... I've treated men with bullet wounds, knife wounds, and shaving wounds. Sometimes the man with the shaving wound gets sepsis and dies from mortification, and the man with the bullet wound lives to see his family again. That, my friend, is fate. The very hand of God, if you will."

Baum shrugged his shoulders and took a puff on his pipe. Exhaling, he again blew a gray smoke ring across the table.

"Well, who am I to argue with God," he surmised. "There may be something to this fate you speak of."

"Glad to see you come to reason, Baum old boy," Blake happily said.

"After all, God did make me handsome and you homely," Baum smiled.

"What?" Blake harrumphed and laughed. "For the love of God!"

A young woman approached the table with a large skillet filled with cut-biscuits. She tossed down a thick cloth on the table and set the skillet on it.

As she turned to leave she stopped and produced from the pocket of her apron a large wooden spoon.

"You'll need this to get them biscuits out of the pan," she said, then moved back towards the kitchen.

Carrigan took another drink from his cup and watched as Baum and Blake helped themselves to the biscuits.

"Eat up boys," Blake said as he shoved a large portion of a still steaming biscuit into his mouth.

The woman arrived again with a pan filled with bacon and eggs. The eggs floated in a thick and gray bacon grease.

"Eat 'em up, fellas, while they're hot," she said as she looked over the table. "Sorry, I forgot your jam."

She quickly moved off to fetch the missing item.

Just like before, Baum and Blake delved into the pan and removed their fill before Carrigan took his serving.

Carrigan noticed the crude way in which the Americans indulged without displaying the simple manners taught to each English child. Taking what he needed, two eggs, and four strips of thick bacon, he sat back and engaged in the conversation.

"Indeed we should be wary. Manassas is a large town and we'll need to keep our wits about ourselves. Fate notwithstanding, we also have Colonel Geary's orders to aid us."

Blake smiled. "Right you are."

The young woman returned and placed a jar of blackberry jam on the table. "I made it not more than a few weeks ago."

As she left, the young waiter from the night before approached the table. He was clean shaven, and his hair newly combed. In his hand was a white apron.

"That information you gentlemen requested," he said. "Among the many people here in the town, there were no injured civilians as of last night. Of the newcomers…"

He paused and looked thoughtful for a moment.

"I asked around, and there are about a dozen or so new folks passing through. Mostly staying at the inns and hotels. But there are many dregs who frequent the brothels and taverns in the east part of town; they come and go without notice," he added.

Baum looked up at the young fellow, then looked across at Blake. "Well, are you going to pay the man for his services?" He shoved a fork full of eggs into his mouth.

Blake produced a silver dollar and handed it to the man. "We appreciate your help. Perhaps you can put this towards a fare to California."

The young man looked astonished as he took the dollar.

"Thank you, sir," he said, his eyes filled with sincere gratitude.

As the waiter left the table silence broke out. Baum and Blake continued to stuff food into their mouths.

Carrigan slowly ate his modest serving. He paused where conversation seemed appropriate, just long enough to sip his coffee, and look around the table.

The several years he lived in the Americas he still didn't quite understand the inhabitants and their customs. Nonetheless, he resigned to not impose his proper English behavior on his friends or acquaintances.

Baum finished and reached for the coffee pot, pouring himself a full cup.

"Well, my fellow patriots, we should gather our goods and be on our way."

Blake swallowed his mouthful of food, and drank the remainder of his coffee. He sat back, producing his pipe, stuffed it full of tobacco, and lit a match.

He puffed on the stem, making the bowl a bright orange. Exhaling the white smoke into the air, he looked over at Carrigan and winked.

"Hope our eating habits didn't upset that John Bull constitution of yours, Carrigan my lad," Blake said and laughed.

"Not at all. When in Rome, and all that sort of rot!" Carrigan chuckled. "But maybe in the future, you might want to pause between gorging, just long enough to make sure that you haven't taken the table cloth and all its contents into your mouth also."

"You are a cheeky fellow, Carrigan my lad." Blake guffawed.

"You've been around us long enough to know that table cloth and all is as good as roast beef and mustard to us colonists," Baum said, then chuckled. "Let's get on that road. Those scoundrels may already be in place waiting to ambush our good Captain as they had done us. But this time, our friend Mister Lincoln may not be so lucky as we three."

Pushing away from the table, Blake stood up, brushed off the biscuit crumbs from his shirt and trousers and straightened his jacket.

"Let's be off then!"

*   *   *

Gumbo burst into the room, his face, a mask of fury.

"Where the hell is that fat tub of shit?" he demanded.

Walter started awake. He'd fallen asleep on the couch and his neck felt stiff.

The girl stirred slightly but didn't come awake. In his hand was the glass of brandy, untouched.

Gumbo and Coffee Cup approached.

"Where the hell have you been? We been expecting you to come back and tell us if Jack were coming or not?"

Walter nodded to the girl in his lap.

"She done fell asleep on me, Gumbo."

Gumbo made a fist as if he was about to strike Walter, but shifted his anger to the girl.

"God damn whore," he said as he grabbed the girl by her thick curly black locks and threw her to the floor.

"It's that damn easy, you fat son-of-a-bitch!" he shouted.

"What's going on here?" The madam emerged from the hallway. She was not pleased and was followed by two very large men, one armed with a shotgun, and the other a pistol. "You the one making my customers concerned?"

"Shut up, you old bitch. I'm here to get my men," Gumbo snapped.

She glanced over her shoulders at her two bodyguards then glared at Gumbo. "You better get the hell out of here or you'll be lying with the trash in the alley."

Gumbo stared at her, his eyes meeting her icy gaze, then he looked over at Walter.

"Get up, let's go."

He walked past the madam, between the two armed men, and into the hallway.

"Jack, you better get to come or be left," he shouted up the stairs.

Gumbo, Walter, and Coffee Cup moved outside, the two guards remained at a safe distance to dissuade any return into the establishment.

Jack stumbled out the door, pushing his way between the two guards. One leg was in his trousers, and he had one boot on.

"Son-of-a-bitch, Gumbo, why the hell you screaming at this hour? I was already on my way."

"Let's get," Gumbo said, disgusted.

The four men headed back into the town and to the livery. They retrieved their horses and walked them to the edge of town.

Once at the town limit, Gumbo climbed atop his horse. "Mount up and let's get this thing done," he said.

Watching his fellow bounty hunters get to their saddles, he took his pistol from his pocket and tucked it into his belt. He pointed his horse down the road towards the railroad tracks and began slowly riding.

"We should be there in about two hours," he said as he took his horse onto the tracks and along a trial that ran to the side. "This trail here follows the tracks to Manassas and up to Devereux Station. Them fellas we aim to meet should be to Devereux Station by daybreak. We'll meet 'em, and be away before they know what hit 'em."

*   *   *

Carrigan arrived at the livery and knocked on the door. Beyond, he heard the voice of a man cursing under his breath. Through the window he saw the illumination of lantern light.

"What in heaven's name is going on here?"

The stable-hand threw open the door. Holding up the lantern he looked out onto Carrigan, Baum and Blake.

"Oh, it's you Yankees. Need your horses, I suppose?"

"We do," Carrigan said.

Shaking his head as if to ward off the desire to sleep, the man scratched his red beard and pulled off his sleeping cap.

"Wait around by the barn door. I'll open 'er up."

He closed the door and locked the bolt from the

other side.

Carrigan, Baum, and Blake moved to where the large barn doors were. The sound of a wooden bar being removed from its brackets was heard, and Carrigan watched as the double doors swung open.

Inside, a lantern hung on a nail in the middle of the room. Stables lined each side of the barn with room for about twenty horses.

Straw covered the dirt floor and the sour smell of horse urine and manure assailed them. In the back, a horse whinnied at the rude awakening. The man with red hair came out.

"Come on, you damned smelly mules, yer masters have come a calling. Yer tack is over there," he said pointing to a set of blankets, saddles, saddlebags, and reins.

"We laid some polish on yer saddles fer ya. All included in your fee."

Carrigan saddle his horse and fixed the reins. He watched as Baum and Blake did the same, then re-tightened the saddle belt; he knew that the horse was holding his breath while fitting the saddle.

"Sneaky old beast," he said to the horse.

"Thank you kindly," Blake said to the stable-hand as he climbed into the saddle.

Carrigan put his foot into the stirrup and climbed up and gripped the reins. "We'd best get a move on," he said.

In the distance Carrigan heard the chirping of frogs and crickets. The gentle sound of the wind in the trees was somehow comforting.

As they made their way along the main road towards the end of town, the smell of smoke from kitchen fires filled the air and mingled with the sweet smell of the forest.

"About an hour or more I think until we get to Manassas," Baum said.

"Make your pistols ready," Blake ordered over his shoulder.

Carrigan unhooked the flap of his holster, took his pistol out and tucked it into his belt.

"I sure hope that Mosby's men are still lurking around Middleberg and haven't drifted over towards Manassas."

Carrigan looked from side to side.

"That makes two of us," Baum added.

CHAPTER 15

The morning light crested the distant hills. Along the way there were plenty of shadows that stretched across the dirt road making the dark mud even darker.

Traffic moved in both directions as Federal troops and citizens came and went along the road. Military wagons carried supplies south and teamster wagons headed east towards Manassas. Gray clouds drifted through the blue sky.

The ride into Manassas was uneventful. Carrigan, Baum, and Blake went directly to the telegraph office at the rail station.

Blake boldly strode up to the door, and opened it.

"We need to get a priority message to the White House!" he said.

A young private wearing a visor, arm garters and leather wrist guards looked over from his desk.

"The White House?" he said raising an eyebrow.

"Yes, the White House – the residence of President Lincoln! You are aware that we have a president named Abraham Lincoln, right?"

The man stood up and walked over to the counter and pulled out a pad of paper.

"Of course I know. It's just that this is the first time I've been asked to send a telegram to the president."

He picked up a nub of a pencil and looked up at Blake.

"Go ahead."

"To President Abraham Lincoln of these United States, stop. From Major William Blake by order of Colonel Geary, stop. Extreme importance, stop. Plot to abduct or kill Captain Lincoln afoot, stop. Ambush planned for Devereux Station area, stop. Three, Captain LeRoy, Captain Baum and Major Blake are moving ahead to intercept plotters, stop. Will need assistance, stop."

The clerk put down his pencil and looked over the pad of paper. His face was grim as he looked up.

"Good God," he said." Them rebs gonna snatch the President's boy?"

"You can probably see the importance of getting this out right away," Blake intimated, the sarcasm thick in his voice.

"Yes sir, right away!"

The private spun around and grabbed the code sheet. He quickly translated the message into code and then set to tapping out the dashes and dots that made up the message.

After the young man finished he turned to look at Blake.

"You should notify the company commander over at Stone House. I'm sure that he can give you a complement of cavalry."

"Where is Stone House?" Blake asked.

"'Bout two miles outside town. Where Bull Run is."

"Two miles? We don't' have that kind of time! And what do you think will happen when these villains see a host of cavalry milling about where they plan on executing their fiendish plan?" Blake furthered.

"Uh, run away I guess," the private said.

"Yes, run away and they'll be free to try again."

"But you'll be less likely to get killed," the private responded.

Blake looked exasperated and harrumphed loudly.

"Well, yes, I suppose when you put it that way…"

He turned and looked at Baum and Carrigan who were sitting on a long bench.

"Looks as though you've handled this well," Baum stated. "So, we should be off then?"

"Of course. If we have to wait for some commander to read our letter, authorize troops and accompany us to Devereux Station, Captain Lincoln will be having tea with Jefferson Davis," Blake explained. "Now, let's get the hell out of here."

The road towards Devereux Station had a steady stream of soldiers and equipment moving in both directions. Along the side of the road at regular mile intervals.

Each checkpoint was made from several covered wagons lined side by side, and a large white canvas tarp supported by poles.

As Carrigan passed one of the checkpoints he saw the soldiers sitting, and watching the traffic pass from under the tarp. They seemed to have little care.

When a civilian wagon tried to pass, the men got

to their feet, approached, halted it, and began searching it.

"Any contraband?" one soldier asked, as the other stood near the horses with his rifle cradled in the crook of his elbow.

Turning his attention back to the road, Carrigan watched as groups of soldiers passed him. They appeared fresh; their uniforms dusty but not torn or worn thin with travel.

Most of the soldiers gave a greeting as they passed the people going in the opposite direction. On occasion, when a woman was passing by, the men tipped their hats and said a hearty, "Good morning, ma'am," or "Pleased to see a pretty face," or "Will you marry me?"

Carrigan smiled. He felt a strange calm and warmth at seeing these men. With the war winding down, those men would be in support roles most likely.

Each man that passed was armed with the new repeating rifle, and the officers who passed looked green and untried by battle. Lucky men, to be spared the horrors of battle.

After an hour, the traffic became thicker with the military ranks being matched by farmer buckboards and women in buggies; all driving towards Devereux Station or on to Alexandria.

Ahead the train station was visible; a simple wooden building painted red with large black letters that read 'Devereux Station'.

Carrigan saw a massive locomotive at rest; the engine parked just below the water tower. The length of the train was not long, twenty cars, half of which were flatbeds carrying artillery and caissons.

Soldiers were visible milling about, some on guard duty, and others standing in the shade of the station roof.

Blake rode up to the station and dismounted. Carrigan and Baum did the same.

The air was filled with the scent of apple pie and bacon, and Carrigan took a long draw of the air. Opposite the station he saw a traveler's inn and tavern; smoke churning from the two chimneys. His stomach growled loudly.

"Good lord!" Baum said while giving Carrigan a wary eye. "Sounds like you're famished."

Carrigan laughed uncomfortably.

"I could do with a nice slice of pie and a cup of coffee is all."

"Do you both mind?" Blake grumbled. "We have a Captain to save."

He waved over a Corporal standing by the train.

"Son, we're looking for Captain Lincoln, where is he?" demanded Blake. "Where can we find him?"

The soldier pulled out of his coat pocket watch and opened it.

"Seems to me that he'd be having a meal over at the public house about now."

"When is the train leaving?" Carrigan asked.

"In an hour. Them engineers need to oil the parts, stock up on some coal, and water the beast down," he said.

Blake turned and began moving towards the tavern. Smoke churned from the train's engine-stack and floated across the dusty road.

The harsh odor of sulfur filled Carrigan's nose as he, Blake, and Baum were enveloped in the blinding haze. Carrigan coughed several times, and his eyes watered.

A shot rang out and shouts erupted from afar. Carrigan emerged from the smoke to see Blake running towards the inn and tavern.

The sound of horses galloping away was heard, and several more shots rang out.

"Renegades!" shouted a man from behind the tavern. "They've run off with the Captain!"

"Mount up," shouted another voice.

Rushing around a low stone wall, Carrigan saw a group of riders galloping towards the back of the train, across the railroad tracks, and west towards the woods. In a matter of seconds, the raiders were gone.

Several soldiers ran to their horses, but Blake shouted to them.

"Hold up! I'm Major Blake, you men will come with us. LeRoy, Baum, fetch our horses. Who's in charge here?"

"Major Hadley, sir," a soldier wearing sergeant stripes called back.

"Go and get him and bring him here now."

"Yes, sir!" The sergeant dashed off towards the train.

Hadley came rushing over. His black leather pistol belt was unfastened, but held in both hands as he strapped it around his waist.

He stopped in front of Blake and quickly secured his belt."What the hell is going on here?" he demanded.

"Sir, some renegades ambushed Captain Lincoln and made off with him," the sergeant explained. "We were fixing to give chase when this Major here halted us and asked to speak to you."

Blake casually handed over the letter from Colonel

Geary. "Read this," he said. "I'll need to commandeer some of your men. Those scoundrels are heading for Goose Creek Bridge, and we can't let them get the Captain into Rebel hands."

The Major looked up, and then motioned with his hand.

"Wendell, Buffus, and Cork— you three ride with the Major. I'll get together some cavalry from the train and follow."

Major Hadley turned and started to walk quickly back to the train, but stopped and looked back at Blake.

"I'll send a telegram to the Manassas post at Stone House. Keep an eye out for fresh troops, they'll be coming post haste!"

He turned and walked on shouting orders.

Baum climbed into the saddle and removed his pistol from its holster. He checked the cylinder, then set the hammer over one empty chamber and replaced the weapon into its container.

Blake stepped into his stirrup and rose to the saddle. Carrigan did the same. Blake raised his hand and motioned forward, then took off at a trot.

"We'll take the road to Manassas and head them off at that meadow we saw," he shouted. "They'll have to cross there to get to Goose Creek. It'll take 'em a half hour longer to get there traveling through the woods."

Blake galloped onto the main road heading back towards Manassas. Carrigan, Baum, and the three soldiers followed in close pursuit.

Dust rose from the horses' beating hooves as the soldiers raced past guard posts, farmers, and military convoys.

"Make way," shouted Carrigan as he took up the position behind Blake.

Soldiers were along the road as they rode on. It began to drizzle; still they rode on. Looking down he saw the exhausted horse, sweat pouring from the horse's skin turning a frothy white.

Rounding a corner the Manassas signpost came into view. Carrigan followed Blake towards the livery.

Pulling up wildly, Blake leapt from the saddle and entered the open double doors of the structure. He called for the stableman.

Carrigan climbed down from his horse. He walked over and scooped up the reins of Blake's animal and led the two beasts to the watering trough. Both horsed dipped their noses into the cool water and drank deeply.

"Unfasten your tack and let's get saddled up!" Blake called out as the stable hand came out and looked the soldiers over.

Two black men came from the stable with two horses each. Blake, Baum, Carrigan and the three other soldiers removed their tack from their respective horses and waited for new mounts.

It only took a moment for six equine to be presented. Quickly they saddled up and readied to ride.

"Hold our steed until we return and we'll give you these animals back," Blake told the liveryman.

"Them horses be my private property, don't let none of them get killed or the Army's going to hear about it," the man threatened.

"Ho," Blake shouted as he rode off towards the northern part of the town.

Closely following, Carrigan saw Blake's

determination. His shoulders were set, he rode high in the saddle at a trot, and he bristled with contempt.

Glancing back he saw Baum, reins held tightly, his cavalier's hat pulled down and his eyes fixed on the road ahead.

The traffic along the road to Gaines was now light. They passed a few Army convoys; the large wagons took up most of the dirt road.

Blake led his men to the side and down into a dry ditch that was cut next to the highway. Once passed, they galloped onto the road again.

The city limits appeared, and Blake charged through a group of women sporting freshly fluffed dresses. Carrigan passed and saw one of the women getting back up after falling.

"Damn Yankees!" she yelled after them.

Through the streets and past several homes they went. Blake slowed, navigated between two fences, then up into the woods.

He made his way through the trees, allowing his horse to walk. They trod through, until they came to a set of breast works.

Leaves had fallen into the ditches, but they were still clearly visible as defensive emplacements. Empty boxes of ammunition, the butt of a rifle and the torn arm from a confederate coat all lay half buried under dirt and leaves.

Blake navigated through the trenches, and then raised his hand to halt. He dismounted and took up the reins of his horse, walking up and over the lip of a trench.

Carrigan followed, as did the rest. Halting, it was clear that they were at a broad meadow surrounded by forest.

Baum came up alongside Blake.

"To make haste to get to Goose Creek by tonight they'll have to cross this here," Baum said as he unraveled his map and laid it over his saddle so it draped down on one side. "See, the location of Goose Creek Bridge is here to the southwest of the meadow. The renegades will probably come from over there." He pointed at a thickly wooded area directly across from them.

"Then we need to be over there," Blake said pointing to the southwest.

They maneuvered through the forest staying well within the perimeter of the trees. Carrigan saw the detritus; it covered the ground like a rug.

From time to time he noticed a rabbit, or raccoon lurking near brambles or briars. A slight breeze made the winds rustle the leaves.

Blake held up his hand and they all stopped. From here, Carrigan saw the opposite side of the glade, and where they thought the scoundrels would come from.

Turning to one of the soldiers, Blake spoke softly.

"What's your name, son?"

"Lloyd Parker Buffus, sir," the young man answered.

"Do you think you can find your way back to Gaines and then back here again?" Blake asked.

"Sure 'nuf, sir. When I lived in Kentucky I hunted in woods just like this," Buffus stated.

"Good. Now move quietly back to town, find the detachment that's supposed to meet up with us and bring them here. Tell them to be stealthy."

"Stealthy?" Buffus said looking confused.

"I mean quiet and out of sight," Blake added.

"I'll be as quiet as a possum up a tree, and I'll be

back faster than Peter jack rabbit," Buffus said.

"If them scoundrels come while I'm gone, keep a few of them renegades alive for a hanging. I do like a good hanging," Buffus said.

Buffus took his horse by the reins and began moving away through the woods.

Blake turned to the others.

"Now, how shall we bottle up these fiends without getting the good Captain killed?

CHAPTER 16

Gumbo halted his horse. He dismounted and removed his pistol from his belt. Something felt wrong.

Coffee Cup also dismounted and pulled down the Captain. The man was draped over the saddle.

The Union Captain was a man of tall stature and heavy build. His blue uniform with its brass buttons made him look like a gingerbread man.

Coffee Cup stared him in the eye.

"You try and run and I'll kill you with a knife," he said. "Now just stand here."

He fished out a pair of wrist shackles from his saddle bag and put them on the Captain. Locking them into place, he put the key into his vest pocket. When he was done he walked over and stood next to Gumbo. "What ya think?"

Gumbo looked concerned. "Them blue coats ain't that fast, but I got a feeling in my gut," he said. "Coffee Cup, fetch yer horse and take a little ride across that meadow. When ya make it to the other side wave your kerchief. Keep your rifle handy."

Coffee Cup went back to his horse and stopped.

"Who's taking the good Mister Lincoln here with them?"

"He'll ride with me," Gumbo said.

Coffee Cup mounted and laid low in the saddle to avoid some tree branches, then took his horse into the open. He recognized the meadow; they'd ridden across it the day before.

He rode slowly, keeping an eye out for any movement in the woods ahead. The last thing he wanted was for a stray farmer or a group of hunters to stumble across them.

Finally, at the other end, he entered the forest and looked around. He dismounted and tied his horse to a tree bow. Stepping out into the open, he took his kerchief from his pocket and waved it in the air.

*   *   *

Blake watched with his field glasses. The man crossing the open field was indeed one of the men they were after. He was moving cautiously.

"Should we open up on 'em?" whispered Corporal Wendell.

"No, let him draw out the others. Remember, we need to catch them in such a way as to not put the Captain in a crossfire."

"Right," Wendell said.

From where the first rider came from, three more emerged. The lead horseman was riding tandem.

Through the field glasses Blake could see a Union officer in the saddle riding just in front of one of the outlaws. They were too close; no shot could be fired unless the Captain were to fall from the saddle.

"Blake…" Baum said. "We can at least even our odds by shooting two of them."

Blake considered this for a moment, then he felt the ground shaking slightly. In the air was a sound like distant thunder.

The men in the middle of the meadow looked up at the spotty clouds in the sky. One of the men, a stocky fellow, seemed confused and shrugged his shoulders.

Then the man riding with Captain Lincoln turned his horse to look the way that they had come.

Through the forest burst a Union Major leading a cavalry charge, his saber pointed out in front and a cry rising into the air.

"Take the fight to the enemy!" he shouted.

Blake turned his glasses on the lead man. It was Major Hadley. Behind him were twenty mounted soldiers with lever action rifles at the ready.

He turned his glasses on the renegades. Several shots were fired. Smoke came from the rifle of the rogue man in the tree line.

The man who rode with Captain Lincoln turned his horse and bolted for the trees. The other men became confused. One of the men's horses reared up, and he fell from the saddle. Another, a stocky fellow, somehow turned his horse and rode after Lincoln.

"Confound those blasted idiots!" Blake cursed loudly.

"They're going to make for that bridge. Let's get going!" Blake shouted. "Mount up and let's go!"

*　　*　　*

Jack hit the ground with a thud and was stunned. The sound of charging hooves was growing louder.

He stood up with his Colt revolver in his hand, aimed, and unleashed only a single round before being hit by rifle fire. The impact sent him to the ground, clutching his chest.

Walter saw what looked like a wall of blue on brown horses coming at him. His heart leapt into his throat, and he pulled hard on the reins to turn his horse towards the forest.

Several bullets whistled by his head and body and he felt as though this was it—judgment day was upon him. He kicked hard at the side of his horse and it bolted towards the tree line, bullets smashing into the branches on either side of him.

Gumbo was just ahead, crashing through the underbrush in a desperate attempt to flee. The Union Captain was struck in the face by a low branch.

Gumbo held him in the saddle to keep him from falling off. From behind he heard the rumble of the soldiers in hot pursuit.

They rode for some time, dashing down ravines, moving through creeks, and taking switch-back deer trails to avoid capture. If they were to be caught, Walter had no illusion that they would be hung after a short trial.

Soon, Gumbo led them up onto a ridge that overlooked a gulley. Here they were able to hide their horses, dismount, and take some water.

The horses were lathered with sweat and probably wouldn't last much longer if they had to go on. The beasts lapped up the water that the two men provided from their canteens.

Walter waited in silence for Gumbo to speak... he knew better than to say anything under these circumstances. For the time being, he was content to watering his horse.

"Walter," Gumbo said. "I want you to ride ahead. Move quietly and slowly, but keep moving until you get to that barn we hid out in. Once there, you'll find a red bit of cloth in a feeding trough. Hang it from the northern eve, and wait for me."

"You'll not get away with this," Captain Lincoln said. "Even if you kill me, the whole Union Army will be looking for you both, and they'll hang you."

"Shut up, Mister Lincoln. The people who paid me will be none too concerned if I arrive and you're missing your tongue," he said. "If I were you, I'd hope them fellas just want to ransom you."

The shackles rattled as Captain Lincoln lifted his hands, retrieved his handkerchief, and mopped blood from his face. Walter walked over and offered the man some water.

The Captain looked up, his eyes black from his broken nose. He nodded at Walter and drank from the canteen.

"Walter, you black sack a guts," Gumbo said with disdain. "You's so stupid you could get a gold brick and trade it for a can a lard." He shook his head. "Don't forget who's payin' you, so get along."

"I'm gettin', I'm get'ing'," Walter said, letting the insult drop.

He took his horse by the reins and headed out. The woods of the area were familiar, and he knew how to get back to Goose Creek and Prichard's barn.

Part of the night he walked his mount, allowing the poor animal to get some rest. The other part he rode, but slowly.

By morning he was near the bridge and was down in the rocky creek bed. The water was low, and he loved the smell of clover and wet sod along the estuary.

Near the bridge there was a path that led up to the road, and he took it. At the top of the path he pulled out onto the road and headed north towards the pasturelands and the large old barn they had used a few days before.

Slowly he moved past a fence line and into the green pasture. He could see some cows meandering about, eating the dark green clover, white buds, and wet grass.

Once down at the barn he went inside. For a moment he looked around at the dusty wooden beams and dirt floor.

Just a few days before, they were all together: him, Gumbo, Coffee Cup, Billy, and Jack, all alive and well. Now only he and Gumbo were alive, or at least as far as he knew.

He searched the feeders and found a large swatch of red cloth. Taking it outside, he moved to the north side of the building. A ladder was lying in the dirt and he took it up and laid it against the side of the barn.

Climbing up, he hung the cloth from the eves and then retreated back inside. At least he could get a few hours of sleep. Surely it would be that long until Gumbo would arrive with the Captain.

Folding his arms over his ample belly, he soon drifted off to sleep.

*   *   *

"Is this a pig for slaughter?" someone said.

Walter woke with a start and reached for his pistol only to find it missing. Standing there were four men dressed in the gray uniform of the Confederacy.

One man held Walter's pistol by the barrel, and in his other hand was a lever action rifle.

"Where's Captain Lincoln?" a man with golden chevrons on his arms asked.

Walter got to his feet. "Uh?"

"Didn't I tell ya he'd try and grab for the pistol?" one of the other men said.

"True 'nuf," said the man with the chevrons. "Now, again, you put up the banner, where's the Captain?"

"He's with Gumbo," Walter blurted.

"Gumbo?" asked one of the other men.

"He's the boss of these fellas," commented the man with the chevrons.

"Gumbo has 'em — and he's heading here," Walter said, trying to hide his fear. "He asked me to come and hang out the banner. Can I have my gun back?"

The man with the gold chevrons looked at Walter with some suspicion.

"Give him his pistol," he said. "When's he supposed to get here?"

"Anytime now." Walter pulled out his pocket watch, opened the cover and noted it was two in the afternoon. "Anytime," he repeated.

"Okay, we'll be waiting in the woods just to the north. When he gets here, come back out and wave to us. We'll be watchin' and I'll send someone to pay and take the Captain off yer hands."

"What's your name?" asked Walter.

"None of your goddamned business," the man with the chevrons said.

The four men walked to a side door and stepped out into the open air. Walter heard horses slowly plodding away.

He moved to one of the widows and peered out. The four men rode to the northern tree line. They melted away into the cover.

No sooner had they reached the forest then he heard another horse approaching. Quickly he moved to the opposite side of the barn and peeked out.

It was Gumbo and the Captain. He moved outside and hurriedly greeted Gumbo.

"Gumbo, some fellas come and they wanted to know where you was."

"God damn it, Walter, you are gonna get me killed with your stupidity," Gumbo chided while jumping down and helping the Captain dismount. "Take the horse and stable it, then tell me what happened."

Walter brought the horse inside, then excitedly he explained that some Confederates came and wanted him to signal them once Gumbo arrived.

"We may not have much time," Gumbo said.

Walter went out the north door and was surprised to see blue uniforms surrounding the barn. He turned and rushed back inside.

"Gumbo, Gumbo," he cried, a streak of terror climbing his spine. "There're blue bellies out there surrounding the barn!"

"What?" Gumbo asked as he pulled out his pistol and rifle.

"You son of a bitch, they followed you!"

Gumbo pointed his pistol at Walter.

"No, Gumbo, it ain't so," Walter said. "There was no Union soldiers before you came!"

"That's right, Walter. They probably followed Gumbo," the Captain said. "He probably brought them to arrest you."

"Shut up," Gumbo told him, "or I'll shoot you."

"Is that true, Gumbo? Did you bring them Union boys to arrest me?" Walter sounded desperate.

"Don't be a plum fool," Gumbo said. "Them blue boys will hang me surely as you."

"He doesn't respect you, Walter… he thinks you're dumb," the Captain said, goading Walter. "He knows that all he has to do is give you to them and he can walk out of here."

"You ain't doing that, Gumbo – I won't let you," Walter said raising his pistol at the man.

"Can't you see this feller's just pulling your leg? He don't know us, or how long we worked together."

"What about that time in Alexandria, when he left you to take the blame for them dead men in the riverboat?" the Captain said

"Ya, you did that, Gumbo," Walter said.

"He's trying to get at you, leave it." Gumbo looked at Lincoln, "How the hell did you know that?"

"It's well known. Didn't you know?" Lincoln asked.

Gumbo turned back to Walter. "Look out that window."

"Do that and he'll put a bullet in your head," the Captain said.

Gumbo cuffed the Captain to the ground, and then he stopped and looked down.

"How did you know about Alexandria?"

*   *   *

Though the barn looked deserted, Hadley's scout reported back that there were two men in there. Major Hadley's men surrounded it and the detachment of soldiers secured the woods further out. Now it was just a matter of time to get into the barn and save the Captain.

Blake, Baum, and Carrigan moved with Wendell, Buffus, and some of Hadley's other men to within a stone's throw of the barn. They heard raised voices inside… what sounded like an argument.

Blake moved up to the barn wall and saw movement inside through the gaps.

All around the barn were tall weeds and this allowed the men to move undetected all the way up to the window. At the window, Blake listened.

He slowly stood and peeked into the window; there were indeed three men. Moving along the wall he came to a door. Here he heard the dissention brewing within.

Blake and his men staged themselves near the entrance. He pulled on the handle, but it was latched from inside. Motioning with his hands for two of the soldiers to kick in the door, he held his pistol at the ready for the fight that was surely waiting.

*   *   *

Walter knew the Captain was right. Gumbo had mistreated him ever since he was with him.

He'd kill him just as easily as he had Billy. He was a thankless killer, and Walter was not going to take it any longer, or turn his back on the man.

"Damn you, Gumbo," he blurted out.

Gumbo turned to look at Walter. "This aint the time. Them blue coats will burn us out if we don't make a move and soon."

"He's going to kill you, Walter… I'll tell them that you helped me."

"That's it," Gumbo leveled his pistol at the Captain and cocked back the hammer. "Money or no money…"

A shot rang out, and for a moment a cloud of smoke filled the air. Walter stood stunned at the blood.

Gumbo clutched his belly, red fluid pumping out as he stared incomprehensibly at the wound.

"You shot me, you mule skinning son of a whore! I can't believe it, you shot me," Gumbo said.

Walter couldn't believe it either. He stood there, the pistol still smoking in his hand and Gumbo bleeding. For a moment he stared without moving, then he saw Gumbo turn his pistol on him. Walter fired a second time, but instead of one report there were two.

Gumbo fell to the ground, a gaping wound in his neck pumping the last of life's blood onto the dirty floor of the barn. Walter wasn't sure, but he was feeling strangely weak.

He buckled at the knees and fell to the ground. The Captain had a pistol in his hand and Walter looked down at his chest to see it turning crimson.

He blinked a few times, then darkness began to surround him. He felt tired and lay on the scratchy hay at his feet, as the smell of the dried manure filled his nostrils.

Silence was coming, and he felt weary and wanted to go to sleep. As his eyes dimmed he heard voices calling to the Captain.

And then silence.

*　　*　　*

The door came off the hinges, and Hadley's soldiers rushed into the room along with Blake and his men. Surprised to see the two brigands lying dead, Blake lowered his pistol.

For a moment he took in the scene as Hadley stepped into the room. He, too, lowered his pistol and holstered it.

"By craky," he said loudly as a great smile grew across his bearded face. "You killed 'em both!"

The Captain kicked the pistol away from Gumbo's limp and lifeless hand. He bent down and rolled him over looking upon him with what looked to be disappointment.

"The fat one named Walter shot him. I guess he'd had enough of his guff."

"Captain Lincoln," Blake began, "are you hurt?"

The Captain gave a bawdy chuckle. "A broken nose maybe." He looked over at Hadley. "I take it you didn't tell them yet?."

"Tell us what?" Carrigan asked.

"Gentleman, let me introduce to you Mister Alan Pinkerton," Hadley said with a chuckle.

"Who?" Baum looked confused. "This is not Captain Lincoln?"

"No," Hadley stated. "Our agents intercepted a secret message last month that Mosby's men were going to make a play for Captain Lincoln."

He paused for a minute while a private entered the barn and whispered something into his ear.

"Yes, carry on," he said to the man. "Now, where was I? Oh, yes, the subterfuge. We intercepted a communication between Mosby and a man named Curts. They figured if they could get the President's son, they could negotiate a truce."

Hadley paused again and gave a smug grin. "We leaked the information that the Captain would be on that train heading to Gaines, and onto City Point this day. Mister Pinkerton here volunteered to set a trap for our ill-fated rogues. Then, we received your telegram and we knew for certain that they were going to strike." He laughed as his men hauled out the bodies. "They had no idea that we were on to them."

"But, who were they working for?" Blake scowled.

"These two were just a couple of stumble bums, you know… bounty hunters. Mosby's boys hired them," Pinkerton said.

"Where's the real Captain Lincoln?" Carrigan looked concerned.

Hadley smiled wider. "He was delivered to City Point today at noon by boat."

"Did your men get the fellow who was on the other side of the meadow?" Baum asked as he looked around. "The one who crossed the field and fired on you from the tree line?"

"I sent a detachment to fetch him. But I haven't heard yet if they were successful," Hadley said, as he pulled out a pipe from his frock pocket and stuffed it with tobacco.

"Shall we gentlemen?" He pointed out the door with his hand.

They left the barn and stood outside. Hadley looked up to see the red cloth hanging from the eaves. He ordered his men to pull it down and then walked over to where his horse was held by a sergeant.

Taking out a match, he struck it on his saddle and put the burning end into his pipe. He looked thoughtful, puffing away and bellowing white smoke into the air.

Hadley looked out at the northern woods for a moment, then harrumphed, mounted his horse and directed his gaze to Pinkerton. "Mosby is out there somewhere. He'll make the mistake of rattling the wrong wasps nest soon enough." He looked down at Blake. "As for you three, your Colonel has some news for you that might lift your spirits. Oh, none of you should speak of this, we don't want to give them Johnny Rebs any more encouragement."

"So, this was all just a charade?" Carrigan asked.

"In a word, yes."

Pinkerton pulled out his pocket watch and opened the faceplate. "Young Mister Lincoln should be arriving at Appomattox right about now."

"Colonel Geary will be awaiting your arrival, gentlemen." Hadley turned his horse. "We can assume that our business here is concluded."

Pinkerton mounted a palomino and took up the reins. The major looked down at the sergeant.

"Finish up here, see that the bodies are delivered to the undertaker at the next town. Don't dally about, either."

He spurred his horse and both Pinkerton and Hadley rode off towards Gaines.

Blake looked at both Carrigan and Baum.

"Don't that just make the hounds scratch," he said. "I'll be damned if they didn't take us as fools through this whole thing!"

"Don't be so hard on yourself, Blake," Baum said with a laugh. "You've acted a fool your whole life. Someone was bound to take you for one."

All around was commotion going on; soldiers looking through the barn, men searching the woods, a wagon being brought for the bodies.

Carrigan nodded his head as if agreeing to something. "If you don't mind my suggestion, I say that we venture to that boarding house in Gaines and fetch some coffee, tea, and biscuits."

"Capital idea, LeRoy," Blake said smiling finally.

"I second that, old chap," Baum said with a smile. "Perhaps they have more bacon and eggs we might partake of?"

Blake took out his pipe and stuffed it. He lit it and took a puff.

"Perhaps we should see if they have a steak, or even some pie. I've had my fill of biscuits, eggs and bacon for the time being."

They left the area of the barn and marched back to where their horses were. Mounting up, Carrigan took one last look back at the troops. Without another word he steered his horse to the road, and began moving with Baum and Blake towards Gaines.

CHAPTER 17

The war had been over for several months. Carrigan wore a tweed suit topped with a derby.

In his room sat a trunk, two suitcases, a bag with his personal papers, and his surgeon's kit. He rose and walked to the table where a basin and urn sat just below an oval mirror.

Pouring out some water into the basin, he wetted his hands and then dried them on a white linen towel bordered in gold stitching. This would be the last bathing he would perform in Baltimore, modest as it was.

Moving to the door he opened it and waited as several men came to the door. "Take the trunks and suitcases; I'll take the bag," he said to them.

The men began taking the items down the stairs and out to a waiting wagon. It was only a matter of hours now until he would be sailing for Liverpool and home.

The hint of a piece of paper was visible in his jacket pocket. It was the sad news of his father's passing on June fourth, eighteen sixty five.

He now longed to return, to see his father's grave, his estate, and his home in London again. It would undoubtedly be bittersweet.

"Only a matter of time," he told himself. Reaching into his pocket he pulled out the boarding ticket. He took one last walk around the room to make sure he hadn't forgotten anything, then he exited and closed the door behind him.

As he walked down the stairs he thought fondly of his two friends, Blake and Baum. The two men were no doubt up to their necks in some drink, or no good at a brothel. He chuckled at the thought.

The landlady met him at the bottom of the stairs, and he paid her for her kindness with two bits and a soft kiss on the cheek. She thanked him and waved as he stepped out into the street.

He sat in the back of the wagon with his trunks and cases and watched as the town of Baltimore passed by. People moved about the streets shopping or working.

Trolleys passed pulled by horses as well as carts, carriages, and cabs. In the air was the smell of coal fires, and black soot hung over many of the two-story homes.

Finally the teamsters turned down toward the docks. Warehouses and businesses lined the street, and men in suits wearing caps and hats moved to and fro.

The smell of fish was growing, as well as the

stench of the harbor. Finally, the wagon turned onto the docks and they headed toward a steamer at berth.

The large ship sported two paddlewheels on both sides and two large black smoke stacks. It was profound; the image of the new age of nautical travel.

Sailors bustled all around, hoisting cargo onto the ship. Dock workers carried cargo and supplies up the gangplank and onto the handsome ship.

The wagon came to a stop, and Carrigan climbed down. He took out his pipe from his coat pocket and filled the bowl with tobacco. Soon he was puffing away. The rich white smoke exited his mouth, and vanished in the sea breeze.

He watched as the teamsters carried his luggage onto the ship and returned for their tip. He paid them with a gold coin and ascended the gangplank.

The quartermaster looked at his boarding pass and escorted him to his tiny cabin. He thought of his father, and how lonely the several homes he'd inherited would be now.

Inside his cabin, he laid on the narrow bunk. Through the walls was the churning of the steam-powered beast's heart; a melodious sound akin to industrial works going up everywhere. He tried to rest, but the desperate eyes and grim faces of his recent past lingered in his mind.

The bed lurched. Carrigan sat up with a start, his pulse pounding in his ears. He opened his watch and noted it was three o'clock.

Outside the cabin the deck moved to and fro. He staggered to the railing to look at the docks.

The ship lurched away from the boardwalk. There were more than two dozen people with him.

Some of those on the docks waved, others dabbed tears from their eyes. To his delight he spotted two figures among the crowd, Blake and Baum.

"We thought we'd drink to your safe voyage!" Blake shouted at him.

"Actually we were just thrown out of the Golden Feather." Baum laughed uproariously. "And had nowhere else to go!"

"If you ever find yourselves in London…" Carrigan shouted, his eyes welling with some emotion.

"Yes, yes, we'll be sure to look you up," Blake called back. "I hope that the English are easier to practice medicine on than Americans!"

A young porter, not more than fifteen, came up to Carrigan. He looked down on the two men who began dancing hand in hand, much to the shock and amusement of the crowd.

"Sir?" the porter asked. "You're a doctor?"

"I was during the war," Carrigan said with a sigh. "A surgeon."

"You was a sawbones?" The boy looked surprised.

"Yes," Carrigan said with a sardonic smile. "I'm a sawbones."

The ship pulled away, its large paddle wheels spewing oily water onto the docks and crowd. The smoke stacks belched out thick black coal smoke as it lurched out into the bay.

Carrigan walked toward the aft. All the while he watched the antics of his two friends, each waving at him from the docks.

"Farewell, Englishman!" Blake shouted.

"I've heard some Englishman think that we're descended from monkeys," Baum shouted. "Make sure you eat plenty of peanuts and bananas on your trip. Maybe you can work at a zoo when you get back!"

Carrigan saw his two friends, each taking drinks from a bottle and passing it back and forth as Carrigan slipped further and further out to sea. Baum stopped and turned back toward the ship, saluted, then about-faced, and walked on.

The four terrible years as butcher faded further and further away in his mind. From the distance he could see Blake and Baum turn and walk from the docks.

Finally, when the coast was out of sight, he filled his pipe with tobacco, and smoked it until the darkness fell over the ship. The young porter came to him and informed him that the Captain requested that he dine with him.

He laughed gently and smiled at the boy.

"Tell the Captain that this old sawbones would be honored."

"Yes, sir."

The young man moved away and up a ladder. Carrigan looked one last time towards America. He reflected on the last strange event of the war—the Captain Lincoln abduction. He smiled at the thought of two surgeons and a cartographer helping to foil the sinister plot.

Blowing a stream of smoke out into the sea air he turned his pipe over and tapped out the tobacco.

"One day all the horror will be as distant as those faded shores," he said quietly."Until then, strong whisky and a good meal will have to suffice."

He turned and walked into the dining room. The doors closed, and he sat at the Captain's table.

The evening waned as the churning hum of the engines vibrated the ship. The diner plates were removed, and the porters came with brandy and whisky.

The captain looked every bit the role in his white uniform. He pushed himself away from the table and looked over at Carrigan.

"I bet you'll be glad to get back to England," he said.

"Anywhere that I won't have to see the torn limbs and tortured souls of war," Carrigan replied.

"Now, if you don't mind, I'd like to have a bottle of whisky, and when I'm done with that one, I'll have another."

ABOUT THE AUTHOR

Lawrence BoarerPitchford ~
Is the author of such works as Tales of Mad Cows and
Brothels, The Lantern of Dern Blackhammer, Thadius,
and In the World of Hyboria.